IT WAS THE ONLY
THING HE COULD DO.

"Robert, I have a problem," Cort informed his superior, not waiting for the lecture about what time it was. This was business, important business, and it had to be dealt with immediately. "I've been compromised."

"How so?" Robert asked, suddenly alert.

"I've met someone in my investigation whom I cannot ignore, or understand . . . It's a woman."

Robert chuckled. "As though I had not already guessed."

"She showed up at that party last night wearing one of my family's jewels that has been missing for more than sixty years," Cort explained. "She's a nobody, as far as society is concerned. She claimed to know nothing about jewel thieves . . . about any of this. But DePesca's man has already ransacked her apartment, and I can't let her out of my sight, for her own protection."

"And she is probably beautiful, young—" Robert guessed "—ah, to be in the field again . . ."

"I'm serious," Cort growled. It was too important an issue to joke about. "I'm in a compromised position. There's some suspicion attached to this woman, yet I am too attracted to her to think clearly."

JANE BIERCE

Black-Tie Affair

ZEBRA BOOKS
KENSINGTON PUBLISHING CORP.

ZEBRA BOOKS

are published by

Kensington Publishing Corp.
475 Park Avenue South
New York, NY 10016

First printing: September, 1992

Printed in the United States of America

To my sister, Dot,
who is as dedicated to reading romances
as I am to writing them.

Chapter One

Jean Barbour took her invitation from her evening bag and flashed it at the usher. Without making eye contact the young man in formal wear waved a gloved hand toward the hotel ballroom.

Eager to satisfy her curiosity about Casino Night and the wealthy people of Palm Beach, Florida, Jean strolled along the red carpet.

In front of her a swarthy man appraised her with piercing dark eyes. Jean raised her chin and side-stepped him, feigning recognition of someone at the roulette table. She refused to be intimidated by any-one.

As her eyes swept the crowded room, Jean spot-ted the most incredibly masculine back.

The man's tuxedo was impeccably tailored to his broad, square shoulders and narrow waist. As the socialites milled between them, she glimpsed black fabric draping long, well-shaped legs and stopping at highly-polished shoes. The back of his silky, jet-black hair had been precisely styled by an expert barber.

Jean had never felt such an overwhelming, instantaneous urge to touch anyone in her life. Even at this distance she felt an attraction that made her heart race for a moment before she fought to control it.

As he turned slightly, the strain on the taut black fabric over his muscular shoulders revealed he was standing with his arms crossed in front of him. His chin grasped in his right hand, he listened pensively to the shorter, balding man standing at an angle before him.

His companion seemed to be explaining something as he gestured impatiently.

Around Jean swirled the soft whir and clatter of the roulette wheels and the croupiers calling for bets. There was the occasional high-pitched laughter of a woman who was winning, the groan of a man who had lost.

At the far end of the spacious room, an orchestra played Big Band music while glittering women and stuffy men danced the steps they had learned as children in ballroom classes.

Latecomers were greeted with a kiss in the vicinity of each cheek. A photographer in formal dress snapped pictures to freeze their smiles in time.

A waiter in a crisp white coat paused in front of Jean, silently offering her champagne from his heavily-laden tray.

Oh, what the heck! Jean thought and took a glass, hoping her hand was steady enough to avoid spilling the bubbly liquid on her borrowed gown.

When she looked back at the men she'd been

watching, she noticed the bald one was pointing in her direction.

Oh-oh! Jean thought, feeling a clutch of fear in her chest. *Found out already.* But it was a silly reaction.

The man might not have been pointing at her at all, but to the exit behind the nearby baccarat table. Trying desperately to appear nonchalant, she raised the fluted crystal to her lips. But she could not avoid watching the scene before her, her green eyes wide with apprehension.

The man whose back she'd been admiring turned toward her slowly, head tilted slightly, listening to what his companion was saying. His profile showed a classic straight nose, a cleft chin, dark brows below a high square forehead, and a hairline receding ever so slightly. His cheek was lean and tanned, his jaw square.

Jean swallowed the champagne she was unconsciously holding in her mouth, feeling a jolt of reaction that couldn't be blamed on the alcohol.

He was gorgeous.

Then he stared straight at her, one eye narrowing. The other eye might have narrowed, too, but it sported a shiner of heroic proportions. If she could rely on her experience with such things, it was about three days old, still slightly swollen and vividly opalescent. It definitely added interest to an almost too handsome face.

Jean blinked and then giggled, trying unsuccessfully to glance away. *You're taking yourself too seriously again,* she cautioned herself, sipping the champagne once more. She hoped the subtly-bubbling liquid would settle the tight feeling in her midsection. Without thinking, Jean stiffened.

The man's gaze dropped a few degrees from her eyes to the area of her rounded bosom. She sizzled when she realized his interest rested on that portion of her anatomy with such intensity. Although Jean never took her eyes from his face, her hand went instinctively to the brooch that secured the low-cut bodice of her gown.

Maybe he was just noticing the ornate pin, not appraising it or assessing what the brooch aided in keeping from sight. Jean was afraid the flush she felt would be apparent in the partially-darkened room.

She tensed as he squared his broad shoulders and straightened his black bow tie. He moved forward with firm, sure strides and was beside her in moments.

His jaw tensed and he kept his voice low. "Come with me," he ordered from the corner of his mouth, his tone brooking no equivocation.

"What?" Jean asked, thinking she was possibly dreaming . . . undoubtedly mistaken . . . not really hearing what her senses double-checked and confirmed.

His hand clamping the bare flesh of her upper arm, he propelled her ahead of him to the exit, in no way gentle.

Intent on avoiding bumping into the elegant people who milled about the entrance to thc room, Jean didn't have a chance to more than quickly glance at her captor's angry face. She was also concerned not to spill the half-full glass of champagne on Denise's midnight-blue gown.

With a nod toward a stern-looking man behind the hotel's registration desk, her captor pushed her into an office marked Private. The bald man stood guard inside the door when it had been slammed shut.

"Now, suppose you tell me about *that*," the taller man commanded as he left her standing in the middle of the room. He pointed an accusing finger toward the brooch she was wearing, like a challenging rapier drawing aim on a vital point.

He spoke slightly from the side of his mouth, as though imparting a secret. The defect at once distracted her and riveted her attention on his every word.

Jean set her teeth together and reviewed what he'd said, hoping to make some sense of it. She covered the piece of jewelry, which seemed to offend him, with her left hand and felt her heart pound in her chest.

He had to be, even in the strength of the harsh overhead lighting, the most fascinating man she'd ever seen. Perhaps she'd seen handsomer faces that were more perfectly symmetrical, but they were generally attached to men whose minds held little to interest her. There was a spark to the combination of powerful physique, well-formed head, and graceful carriage she had never encountered before.

She reacted with fear. She knew she should not have given in to the temptation that had led her to be at this gala.

In the back of her mind she heard a voice telling her that she'd better just tell the truth and hope for the best. What could he do to her? Send her home from the party? That was the worst that could happen, she realized with relief. Jean had a quarter in the sequined bag hanging from her arm. She could call Denise to come get her a little earlier than midnight, as they had arranged.

"All right," Jean started, after moistening her mouth with a sip of champagne. "I crashed the party. I work as a calligrapher for the printer who engraved the invitations. I addressed the envelopes and did all the other fancy penwork on the programs and menus. I . . . I just wanted to see something like this, just once in my life. So when I reproduced the guest list on a computer at the office, I added my name."

"I don't care about that!" he spouted impatiently, glaring at her and gesturing impatiently. "Don't you know that no one wears the real thing to these events? Anything shining out there that's more than three carats is probably paste because the jewel thieves can smell real ice a light-year away. Haven't you heard that the sharks have been gathering for a week?"

As his jaw set, he pressed blunt fingertips to the blackened area of his left cheekbone. The movement drew Jean's attention to the exquisite lines of his facial structure and the heavy gold ring on his hand, possibly bearing a family signet.

"Real . . . ice?" Jean asked, repeating the only

12

words that had made much sense to her. Then she threw her head back until she felt her long blond hair prickle against her shoulders. "The stones in this pin aren't real! Whatever gave you that idea?"

"Whatever gave me that idea?" he mimicked, reaching his right hand into the breast pocket of his pristinely-tailored tuxedo jacket. He produced a gleaming black leather badge case, which he flashed open at her. He was about to replace it when she reached for it.

"I've always wanted to see something like that," she told him in wonder. Putting her glass on the desk, Jean stayed his hand with a slight pressure of her manicured fingertips on the edge of the leather case. "In every mystery movie I see, people flash their badges so quickly that how's anyone to know you're really a police officer? You don't look — Interpol?"

His mysterious gray-gold eyes looked back at her without flinching.

She backed off and took a long breath. "Interpol. I've stepped into something, huh?"

He replaced the badge in his pocket and squared his shoulders with a serious nod.

"But this pin . . . it's not real. . . ." Jean faltered.

"You little fool!" he spit out. "Who set you up?"

"Set me up? What do you mean?"

"Who told you to come to this party?"

"I decided to come to this party myself," she explained. "Denise — Denise, my roommate — egged me on a little, but it was all my idea. It's . . . it's her gown. I was going to wear her black one, planned to

13

all week, but then at the last minute we decided the color really didn't suit me, so I wore this. I dug out this pin to hold the front together."

"Dug?" he demanded tightly.

"I keep a lot of things in a box . . ."

"Oh!" he exclaimed, his eyes flicking away to the other man momentarily. "She's telling the truth, Rolland."

"Well, you have a built-in polygraph!" Jean shot back, showing her own exasperation. Her right hand went to the brooch to make sure it was still firmly clasped, although she'd taken the precaution of putting a small safety pin in the gown to preserve her modesty should the old piece not hold. "How could anyone think this is anything but a pretty piece of glass?"

He took her hand gently, switching his attention to the two rings she was wearing. On her index finger she had a small creamy-blue opal surrounded by six seed pearls. On her ring finger was a dark rose stone with two small pearls in a rather pleasing if plain swirled setting. He studied each, not noticing that his gentle touch on her palm caused her pulse to do unprecedented dances in her veins.

"I suppose this is all glass and plastic, too, no?" he asked, for the first time his grammar showing a foreign construction to match the very thinnest accent she couldn't place.

"There's a flaw in the center stone of the one ring, and a pearl is chipped in the other," Jean explained, blithely offhanded. "I'm told that keeps them from being truly valuable."

"I have some land west of here I'd like to sell you, my dear," he taunted caustically.

"All right," Jean conceded, gritting her teeth at his sarcasm. "My mother told me this red stone was appraised when she was in high school at two hundred dollars. She had no idea what the other is worth—"

"And you certainly don't, either! How the hell did you—" He looked at her face, then dropped her hand as though it were a burning coal. "I must have a long talk with you. But right now I have to take care of some more dangerous gate-crashers."

Jean felt the corner of her mouth turn up as she centered her attention on the prodigious bruise around his left eye. "Um-hmm!" she murmured cheekily.

"Stay here," he growled, pointing at the long leather couch against the paneled wall.

Jean glanced at the couch, then back at him and raised her eyebrows very deliberately. The look he returned was meant to kill, she was certain. She turned to watch him leave the room, taking his shadow, the bald man, with him.

There was nothing to do but sit down on the couch, sip her champagne, and wait for him to return. This was definitely not how she had expected to spend the evening!

It had been a fun job to do, addressing invitations with the famous names of Palm Beach high society. She hadn't considered Casino Night a charity and neither had Ben Evans, the owner of the print shop that had engraved the invitations on cream vellum. He hadn't even offered a reduced rate because the organization was a high-budget program. If he'd considered it a legitimate fund-raising event, he'd have offered to discount his price by a good percentage.

Jean had seen the woman who had tediously gone through print samples and swatches of paper to choose the style and stock. In her white linen slacks and printed silk blouse, and with her subtly-dyed blond hair smoothed back with a bright scarf, she had carried herself with an air of superiority. It was as though she was condescending to enter the business office. *It's a dirty job, but someone has to do it,* had been written all over her face as she had moved past Jean without acknowledging her presence.

Carrying a can of cola, Jean had sauntered back to the noisy pressroom and looked down at her jeans and oversized man's T-shirt with some amusement. Her clothes were a badge of independence. As a young girl back in a small town in Pennsylvania, she had realized she would never lead a glamorous life.

She'd gone to college to study history, with an eye to becoming a teacher. But during her junior year Jean's mother had died. Suddenly life became disjointed. Her father remarried. And when Jean's boyfriend, Bob, had started talking of changing the direction of his life, she had begun searching for meaning and adventure for herself. That she had eventually come to West Palm Beach was not totally unexpected, given the stories she had been told as a child.

Bits and pieces of her background turned a coin now and then. She'd learned calligraphy as a Girl Scout, and occasionally Ben paid Jean for special projects in addition to her other duties. Few brides wanted to hand-address their invitations these days; few had the patience or legible handwriting that lasted through two hundred envelopes.

The list of names asked to this fund-raiser had amused Jean as she recognized the people from stories appearing in the *Daily News,* the fabled *Shiny Sheet.* Its glossy pages chronicled Palm Beach society parties with pictures of the elegant party goers. Then Ben had shown her the menu that she was to calligraphically transcribe on several sheets of paper to be posted at the buffet tables.

"Boy, I wish I could go," Jean had murmured to herself. And as she had painstakingly drawn the whirls and swirls on the seemingly unending stack of envelopes, a plan developed. Of course, there would be a few extra invitations. If not, she could always leave her desk, go back to the pressroom, and tell Manuel to make up a few. It happened all the time; a couple units might be smudged or wrinkled, the paper marred by an imperfection that, on a job like this, would not be acceptable.

Since the original list had been done on a computer, it was easy to insert her name and address. The job took five minutes during a morning break at Ben's shop. Back at the charity's office, her name would probably be added to the guest list without question.

In moments of wild fantasy Jean wondered if this brazen subterfuge would lead to other invitations.

Then she told her puckish plan to Denise Gibson, her roommate in the cramped apartment over a deli in West Palm Beach. Denise was enthusiastic in her endorsement, throwing all her support into the project and providing the dress.

Originally they had decided on a long black gown with a low-draped neck and lower back line. It was not until Jean had tried it on about seven o' clock that evening that they'd come to an anguished conclusion. No matter how good Jean's tan was or how erect her posture, the dress just did not look right.

Denise had pulled the dark-blue gown from the closet and held it to Jean's shoulders. "The color is great with your skin tone," Denise appraised critically.

"But it's slit to the navel," Jean nearly wailed. The gown was not really that outrageous, but Jean was not prepared to wear anything quite so sexy.

Denise, her vaguely Mediterranean ancestry evident in her olive complexion, liquid brown eyes, and deep brown hair, was of a more earthy demeanor and philosophy.

Having an overwhelming interest in clothes, Denise had found a consignment shop that sold garments previously owned by the elite. The store often took back a dress Denise had worn a few times and gave her credit toward her next purchase. The arrangement allowed Denise a certain panache.

Jean looked from the gown to her roommate and back again, feeling trapped into putting on something that did not make a valid statement about the person she was. She had put the dress on and studied herself in the cloudy full-length mirror on the bedroom door. The cheap silvering of the mirror could not disguise the fact that Jean's well-proportioned chest was in danger of being exposed if she turned sideways.

While rummaging in her bureau drawer for a small safety pin, she opened a battered yellow candy box. It held an odd assortment of possessions, which had always defied organization. There was her great-grandmother's glass and rhinestone brooch, something Jean had been given to play with on rainy days as far back as she could remember.

"Oh, use that!" Denise had urged, tossing her shaggy dark hair over one shoulder and flopping down on Jean's bed. "It will look genuine. At worst, people will think it's another piece of paste. The rich are too afraid to wear real jewelry anyway."

Jean had laid the antique piece aside and kept poking around until she found the safety pin. Once they had agreed on just where the gown needed to be fastened together, she gave in to Denise's insistent prodding and put the old flower-shaped brooch over the safety pin, hoping neither would let her down.

Being essentially a small-town girl, Jean deferred to her roommate's more sophisticated judgment. It was often easier to give in than risk Denise's temper. After all, Jean had been the late-comer, seeking an apartment to share when she arrived in West Palm

Beach. Denise had been welcoming, but on her own terms, and since she had superior knowledge of their surroundings, Jean watched and learned from her.

The gown was a shimmery blue and the big stone in the pin had a sort of yellow tinge, cut like a gumdrop and surrounded by a ring of rhinestones. They were faceted in the usual manner and remained as clearly white as ever.

The piece of jewelry went surprisingly well with the evening dress. Jean carefully studied her overall effect in the mirror. Though she wasn't vain, she wanted to look presentable in a room full of high-class people. On the other hand, she didn't want to attract attention. Jean had felt confident she could mingle unnoticed in a crowded ballroom. . . .

Until she could not take her eyes off one perfect specimen of manhood. Her eyes had probably burned a hole in his back. He was just retaliating for her lack of manners with this absurd story about Great-grandmother Finney's pin being valuable.

Jean set her nearly-empty champagne glass on the coffee table in front of her and stared at the opal on her index finger. It was from her mother's side of the family, as was the other ring. Jean's family had never been able to afford expensive jewelry. The noise that came from her throat was disgruntled and puzzled. Maybe . . . maybe the man was right. All the pieces were old, very old. That was probably why they were valuable.

Her mental processes shouldn't be so affected by one serving of champagne, even though it was in a tulip glass of generous capacity. With this type of crystal, the bubbles were supposed to last longer. It was one of the things she'd learned in the past few years by reading *Southern Living* and *Town & Country.*

Jean wandered about the office, bored, then decided to test the boundaries her captor had set for her. She felt the urge to "powder her nose," so she tried the doorknob and found the room was unlocked.

Cautiously she opened the door and peered outside. No one seemed to be standing guard over her, so Jean took a deep breath and sauntered nonchalantly to the ladies' room at the end of the long carpeted corridor.

The lounge contained a sitting room fitted with mirrors, upholstered armchairs, a divan, and silk greenery in marble urns.

Several elegantly-garbed women were gossiping there, the scents of their costly perfumes mingling with heavy cigarette smoke. Jean drifted through the area without being noticed.

She was washing her hands when she noticed a small, bright-eyed woman surreptitiously transcribing juicy tidbits of overheard chatter into a tiny notebook.

Jean had always been a quick study, and she realized this was probably a columnist for the *Shiny Sheet.* But she studiously avoided letting the woman know she was watching her write down information. Jean had to admit she was curious herself.

There were some catty remarks zinging through

the air, which Jean wished she understood better. Some of the comments were vicious, and Jean knew instinctively the reporter could make someone desperately uncomfortable, if not cause her to flee for her emotional life.

"Well, if I were Piet van Roy, I'd be watching Kiki in her sleep when that handsome cousin of his is around," one woman commented in a deep alto slurred by too much to drink. "Isn't he the most divine thing you've seen in an age?"

The observation set somebody into a fit of giggles, but Jean was busy searching her mind, trying to supply a face for the name Kiki van Roy. Oh, yes, the woman who had spent the better part of a morning choosing the invitations in Ben Evans's office.

Someone else was saying, "It's a pain to have a necklace and earrings duplicated so you can wear them to an event like this. I was telling Lance it's a bore having all those jewels if they just languish in a vault. It was more fun when you could keep them in the dressing table drawer and run your fingers over them whenever you felt the need."

Oh, to be so deprived! Jean thought, looking into one of the mirrors, then checking the clasp on her brooch.

It was time to go back to the office. After all, she didn't want to call any more attention to herself than she had already.

A short while later she was within sight of the office door when her captor strode out, his posture clearly revealing he was intent on finding her.

"Where have you been?" he demanded the moment he spied her. Fire seemed to leap in the depths of his gray-gold eyes. Jean hadn't noticed before how very changeable his eyes were.

"A lady has to powder her nose now and then," she told him coolly.

He studied her nose for a moment, then drew himself to his full height and sucked a hissing breath through his teeth. He waved a decisive arm toward the office, and she felt constrained not to argue with him.

He closed the door firmly behind him. "I've determined it's safe for you to join the party," he declared, "as long as you stay close to me and don't wander off with anyone."

"As offers go, it's better than a sharp stick in the eye," Jean said dryly.

The set of his jaw told her not to press her luck. He held his arm toward her as though he expected Jean to take it. There wasn't an alternative. She placed her hand in the crook of his arm, primly and properly, and strolled forth, head high. His arm was firm and muscular beneath the soft wool of his sleeve.

They turned heads as they entered the ballroom, but Jean was disconcerted that most of the observers were female. Well, why not? She supposed the men were more interested in the money floating around on the gaming tables than in a strange woman.

The object of this slow promenade through the room, Jean realized, was to discourage anybody from getting near enough to her to steal the alleged gem she wore. It was clear this Interpol agent had no intention of settling down to even watch the roulette wheel.

What a bore! Jean thought.

He turned suddenly and tilted his head toward her. "Would you care to see the buffet?" he invited.

"Why not?" Jean returned offhandedly. Frankly, it was the best offer she was likely to get.

From making up the menu sheets, she had some idea of the delicacies that would load the long, linen-draped tables. Still, Jean was unprepared for the display of silver, crystal, and ice sculptures and the fanciful arrangement of the food. Attentive chefs stood by in immaculate white smocks, their tall hats crisply pleated.

"This is what you should be guarding," Jean pointed out in a low aside to her escort as she took a plate and held it out for a slice of beef Wellington.

Suddenly he laughed, a low, hearty rumbling sound that seemed to surround her with warmth.

Kiki van Roy slipped into line behind him, looking up familiarly with her fluttering lashes. She wore something side-draped and shimmery white. A Valentino, Jean guessed. Certainly not a Givency or Oscar de la Renta; yes, Valentino. At Kiki's throat glittered a narrow choker of diamonds and matching earrings dangled from her ears, or at least paste representations of what everyone assumed languished in the van Roy vault.

She had the air of being still a bit too young to have merited anything truly ostentatious from her husband of scarcely ten years.

"Darling, I didn't know you were bringing a date," she cooed.

Ah, the van Roy cousin! Jean realized with a side-long glance from one to the other.

She sensed, with that intuition women have but try to deny, that Kiki had a lustful interest in this man. *As I live and breathe, her husband does have competition,* Jean thought, then hated herself for the twinge of unwarranted jealousy she felt.

"No, we just met," he told Kiki. "I'm afraid I haven't even had a chance to ask her name."

Kiki chuckled pointedly, and Jean understood that not all the cats had repaired to the restroom. "I thought you must certainly be on closer terms than that, the way you were— But of course, you continental types are always taking arms and kissing hands."

Coming to the end of the buffet, Jean turned to drift toward the petite linen-draped dining tables, knowing in her heart she ought to have stayed home. She'd never reckoned with having to maintain a conversation with anyone at this affair, let alone a woman capable of being viciously bitchy.

Jean took a step and was confronted by the gossip columnist. *This time you got yourself into more than you'd bargained for,* Jean thought.

A warm, comforting hand touched her bare shoulder, and she looked up at the van Roy cousin in surprise.

"I see a place over there in the corner where we can sit," he said, pointing it out. Mercifully there were only two little brocaded chairs at the table.

She had to give him perfect marks for being gallant. No matter how stupidly naive he thought her, he treated her like a lady, making certain she didn't drop her plate as she sat down. Well, she wasn't quite that uncoordinated!

"My cousin's wife raises a good point," he said, sitting down beside Jean and adjusting his pant legs over his muscular thighs. "We haven't exchanged names. I'm Cort van Roy."

"I'm Jeanellen Barbour. My friends call me Jean." *Why did I say that! I have no intention of letting him get that close to me!* she thought.

"Then you must call me Cort," he said with a slightly lopsided smile on his well-formed lips.

"If you insist," Jean murmured, trying to decide which of the delicacies on her plate to try first.

He turned his attention to his own food and to the people who moved past them.

She took stock of their position. They were sitting in a corner against a wall, where no one could surprise them from behind, just like the gunslingers in an old Western movie, she thought.

Cort van Roy's eyes constantly scanned the room. Although he seemed to be enjoying what he was eating, he was more interested in the flow of people.

Once in a while Jean thought he would say something to her, but he always seemed to think better of it. Frankly, he wasn't good company, she appraised. She had the feeling he wanted to talk to her but didn't know what to say.

His English had certainly seemed fluent enough when he berated her for her stupidity. Actually, there wasn't anything Jean wanted to talk to him about, either. She prayed for the witching hour to come when Denise would pick her up out front and she could go home. This excursion into the society world had not exactly been a stellar occasion.

Cort handed his empty plate to a waiter, who seemed to appear at just the right moment. Then Cort whisked two glasses of champagne from the tray of another waiter, who also materialized as if on cue. He handed a glass to Jean and took a sip from his own.

Jean disposed of her plate and settled back in her chair, thinking she had better make some quick mental notes of the clothes the women around the room were wearing. Denise would demand detailed descriptions. Jean's scrutiny was interrupted when Cort cleared his throat pointedly and got to his feet.

"Will you please come back to the manager's office with me?" he asked politely, but without giving her a chance to refuse. "We must discuss what we are going to do with the fortune you are wearing on the front of your gown."

At first he made it clear she should take his arm. But when they reached a small knot of people, he placed his hand lightly on her shoulder, his fingers curling slightly over the edge of her collarbone.

Jean was terribly conscious of the pressure and warmth he exuded. Suddenly she was experiencing a difficulty in breathing she had not noticed before.

A few moments later he closed the door of the office behind them once more and stood squarely in front of her. "I think it would be best if you left the

27

brooch in the hotel safe. And the rings—"

"No," Jean protested, backing away from him.

"I'll give you a receipt," he promised.

"What good would that do?" Jean asked, her mind grasping at straws.

"I'm bonded," he stated. "If something happens, you'll be reimbursed the value of the gems. My dear, you just do not understand—"

"I've never had any trouble before."

"Jean, there was a very notorious international jewel thief just outside the door this evening. He works with an equally-dangerous accomplice. I was able to have him detained for trespassing, but I do not expect that to sidetrack him for very long. Now, if you want to avoid my recounting the horror tales of some of his victims . . ."

Jean stifled a gasp. While she pondered the gravity of the situation, greatly hampered by the intensity of his multihued eyes and the forceful set of his jaw, Jean backed up another step. But her retreat was blocked by a carved antique armoire.

Trapped. There was no other place for her to go. Cort's long fingers reached for the brooch and went about unpinning it with absolute authority, to say nothing of distractingly-intimate contact with the overheated flesh of her bosom.

To her credit, she did not gasp. She knew the bodice would not spring open and breach what modesty she had left. After all, she'd been a Girl Scout. She was prepared.

Chapter Two

Cort drew a ragged breath as he slipped the pin from Jean's gown. He'd wondered what he would do when he was inevitably exposed to what must be supremely-elegant flesh. He vowed he would be a gentleman. He would look directly into Jean's fascinating green eyes and apologize, at least overtly, for having to remove the diamond brooch.

When the front of the evening dress stayed securely where it was, he didn't know whether to be disappointed or relieved.

He raised his chin, squared his shoulders, and turned toward the desk. His hand fumbled in his pocket for his jeweler's loupe, barely able to keep the magnifying eyepiece from falling onto the blotter. Composing himself, Cort lifted the loupe to his right eye and studied the gem.

It was a damned inconvenience to have to use his right eye since his left one was dominant. But it still hurt from his encounter with Stefano De-Pesca earlier in the week, and the tender flesh would not tolerate the strain of holding the glass.

A sigh of appreciation escaped him for in his hand was indeed the van Roy Champagne Rose diamond. It had been smuggled in its raw form from the Transvaal during the Boer War by Claus van Roy, hidden in Amsterdam for years before it was carried to New York City by Ernst, Claus's son, and cut to be mounted and presented to Ernst's wife, Ruta.

The official account of its disappearance was that it had been stolen from their New York residence in February 1925 as the family holidayed in Palm Beach. But Cort had never believed that story because his own grandfather, Jan-Wilhelm van Roy, told him not to.

The pale but even champagne color of the diamond was a rare coloration, adding mystery to the fire deep in the unique double-rose cut of the stone. Weighing about eight carats, the van Roy Champagne Rose was shaped somewhat like a gumdrop to maximize the rough crystal it had been cleaved from. It was surrounded by a ring of twenty brilliant-cut white diamonds, not nearly as valuable as the center stone, but meticulously matched and probably totaling another three or four carats. The gold setting was that of a rose, if one looked at it a certain way and knew its history. The clasp was hidden behind the leaves, and the piece was designed to be worn with the blossom downward, as Miss Barbour—Jean—had done so correctly.

Only someone with Cort's training could really

appreciate the rarity, the elegance, the perfection of the piece, so painstakingly assembled by a master smith. This stone, in the gem trade termed an "outsider" because of its lack of documentation through bills of sale and customs records, had eluded Cort for so long that he had almost been convinced it no longer existed. He had many times given up the quest, only to be spurred on again by the memory of the portrait of Ruta van Roy wearing this exquisite jewel.

It was because of the brooch's distinctive style and his avid interest in finding it that Cort had recognized it so readily at a distance. It had taken him a moment to sort through his disbelief at its being there, on the front of a gown that was not terribly haute couture.

In that moment he had felt a clutch at his heart and his mouth had gone dry, his lips tingling. During a second glance he had seen the total woman, the slender figure, the proud stance that, he realized in an instant, challenged his attention. God! What had she thought of him!

And right behind her was Stefano DePesca. Cort knew he had to keep her from turning away, had to keep DePesca from seeing that stone if he had not already seen it. Detective Rolland, Cort's liaison with the Palm Beach Police Department, had at first thought he was insane for bolting across the room and hustling the woman into a private office. But it was the only way to keep the gem and the woman safe.

Now Cort could not take his eyes away, turning the jewel one way and then another to make the fire dance. Although the piece needed an expert's attention to clean it properly, it was breathtaking as it stood, cherished in his tingling fingertips.

"Well?" Jean demanded impatiently, braced against the desk with her fists almost digging into the polished mahogany surface.

Where his eyes first glanced was the place the brooch had originally reposed. *This will not do,* he scolded himself, allowing the loupe to fall into his hand as he looked into her green eyes.

"It is indeed the van Roy Champagne Rose," he stated, conscious of the slight tremor in his voice. "It was reported stolen some time ago."

"It belonged to my great-grandmother," Jean contended, her eyes flashing some of the same fire as the diamond, not allowing him a shred of credibility. "She had it for a very long time. I can't believe it was stolen . . . that she stole—Well, surely there's a statute of limitations. Besides, she died in the early seventies."

"Of course there is a statute of limitations!" Cort assured Jean, replacing his jeweler's glass in his pocket. "At this point, the possessor is the legal owner. Which places you in some jeopardy, Miss Barbour. It's worth a lot of money, and you can't just keep it in a cigar box—"

"Candy box," Jean corrected haughtily.

Cort waved his hand. "The safest place for it is in a safety-deposit box here in the hotel," he told her, placing the brooch in the middle of the blotter. "I'll give you a receipt for it. And your rings."

"Whoa!" Her eyes blazed. "A lot of money?"

"I have no idea what the opal is worth until I study it," he explained. "Opals are brittle, prone to shattering. An antique one is rare, especially if it is in the original setting. Its value might be . . . much higher than you would be comfortable with. As for the other stone, I can't even tell what it is until you take it off."

"Take it off!" Jean exploded. "Not a chance. I'd feel naked without it."

Her bright eyes challenged his, yet when he reached for her hand, she did not resist. He took the opal ring from her index finger and studied it without the benefit of his glass. She retreated, and Cort knew she had no intention of letting him close to the other ring.

He had to make a decision. He could not make an issue of taking it, too, if she was so adamant. Perhaps it was not worth very much; perhaps she liked it merely for its attractive lines and sentimental value. He would not press the matter.

"I assume you must have more jewelry at home," he posed, looking for something to write on.

"Yes. Oh my God! Denise will be leaving in a few minutes to come pick me up." Jean told him, reaching for the telephone. "Should she wait?"

"Tell her you will be escorted home," Cort instructed tightly.

There was no way he was going to let Jean Barbour out of his sight until he had inventoried the contents of her cache at home, not with the likes of DePesca and his henchman, Simon, roaming the streets.

Cort prepared a receipt with his most precise penmanship and handed it to her.

The color left Jean's face when she saw the amount he had appraised the gems. She retrieved the champagne glass from the coffee table, but there was not a drop to moisten her lips.

He studied her face for a long moment, afraid that after all the years of roving the world, searching for the men who traveled the "outside" of the gem world, he had met a deceptively-clever nemesis.

What if she had come into possession of the Champagne Rose by less than honorable means? What if she had made up the story? Could he, would he, deal with her as he had other criminals? Even as Cort contemplated these discomforting thoughts, he was conscious of his left eye throbbing dully. It was probably because he was tired.

While Jean called her roommate, he found an envelope into which he slipped the jewels, then summoned the night manager into the office. Quickly Cort explained that he needed to put something into the vault.

Jean reluctantly witnessed the transaction and placed the receipt in her sequined evening bag. Perhaps it was fatigue that dulled her hostility.

Cort sent a hotel employee to collect Jean's wrap from the checkroom. Then he called for his driver to bring the limousine he had hired for the evening around to the side door of the building.

Jean draped her black velvet evening shawl around her tanned shoulders and looked back at him challengingly.

Cort found the short walk to the car taxing. It had already been a very long week, and he certainly didn't need this unexpected complication, delectable though the principal appeared.

Jean was not prepared for the silver-gray, chauffeur-driven vehicle that rolled to the curb outside the manager's entrance. A hotel employee held the car door for Jean and Cort as they got inside and settled into the back seat.

"Tell my driver how to reach your home," Cort ordered, wearily stretching his legs in front of him. Jean leaned forward to confer with the chauffeur, a swarthy young man who looked as though he could defend himself against all comers. He acknowledged her instructions with a nod. "Near the Freeman Deli?" he asked.

"Over it, to be honest."

"Best corned beef in town." He chuckled softly as he winked into his rearview mirror.

"What can you tell me about Simon?" Cort asked his driver, cutting into the first comfortable moment Jean had experienced all night.

"He hailed a cab when I started the car," the driver told him. "I thought he might be following us, but I don't see him anywhere now.

Cort rested his hands on his knees. "I suppose this is as good a time as any for an explanation of what has happened," he said with a sigh, not looking at Jean but somewhere beyond the confines of the car.

Jean chuckled. "Truly."

"I came to Florida to spend my holiday with my cousin and his wife," Cort explained slowly. "But at a marina, where I tied up to get some fuel, I chanced to encounter a jewel thief whom I have been tracking for several years. I tried to waylay him, but as you see, he got the best of me."

Jean looked at Cort's blackened eye sympathetically. "Too bad."

"I checked in with my superior in Paris, and he authorized me to work with the Palm Beach police to set up a plan to catch him. We felt our best chance was at Casino Night, which was already being covered by the police anyway. We went to a lot of trouble to set up an elaborate plan to trap DePesca. That, Miss Barbour, is what you interrupted this evening."

"I'm sorry," she murmured contritely.

"We dressed a lovely young policewoman in a designer gown and borrowed some outstanding jewelry for her to wear," Cort explained. "She was waiting outside in this very car for the signal to enter the hotel when you arrived. You walked right past our quarry and stopped not two meters past him, picked up a glass of champagne, and stood there like an invitation to be robbed."

"I assure you, that was not my intention," Jean said, gasping.

Cort cleared his throat. "I had to act quickly to remove you from the scene. And when I walked past the thief with you, I realized that he knew we had set a trap. I had to call off our operation immediately and hope our decoy would be able to return to the stationhouse safely."

"And did she?"

"Yes. My man José saw to that," Cort said, reaching over the back of the seat to give the driver a pat on the shoulder.

Jean did not realize she was being gauche to invite the chauffeur up to the apartment along with Cort until Denise maneuvered her into the kitchen and told her. Jean merely shrugged. If Cort was uncomfortable with the situation, it would repay him for the uneasiness he'd caused her.

Denise quickly prepared a pot of coffee and poured four cups, then followed Jean into the bedroom. She discovered Jean searching her dresser drawer for the candy-box cache. "My, my, my, you made good use of your evening!" she whispered cheerfully. "I assume you're interested in the one in the tux."

"I'm not interested in him!" Jean denied, but

she knew neither she nor Denise believed a word.

"What happened to your pin?" Denise asked, suddenly shocked into concern. "And your opal ring! Jean!"

"He made me leave them in the vault at the hotel." Jean sighed. Then she lowered her voice and spoke very slowly. "He's from Interpol, Denise. A gem expert. That . . . brooch was the real thing. And the ring."

Denise stared, her jaw dropping slightly in disbelief. "How —"

Jean shrugged. "I don't know."

Jean rummaged through the box, removing odd buttons and her small sewing kit before taking it to the dining table. At a nod from Cort the chauffeur went and stood by the door with his feet slightly apart, his arms crossed over his chest.

After giving Jean a look that told her what he thought of the careless way she looked after her jewelry, Cort sat down at the table. His jacket hung open slightly, revealing that he was carrying a small pistol in a holster under his left arm. Jean swallowed uneasily and pretended that she hadn't noticed it.

"I need a piece of paper," Cort requested as he looked at the contents of the box. "Perhaps two."

As time ticked by, Jean grew weary of watching him inventory and draw precise diagrams of the pieces of jewelry she'd inherited from her great-grandmother, her grandmothers, and her mother. She wished that he would put every piece in the pile aside. She knew they were just junk and he couldn't have any interest in them.

But he took agonizing care to study, describe, and evaluate the entire collection of pins and un-matched earrings Jean had toted around the coun-tryside for years.

When it seemed he had finally completed the task, he looked up at her. "This is not everything you own," he challenged. "I know that women have school rings, little lockets their fathers gave them. Perhaps you have some items such as these?"

"A few things," Jean conceded, getting to her feet, grateful for a chance to move after sitting at the table watching him for so long. "I'll get my jewelry box."

"No!" he stopped her. "Don't you know any-thing! You ought not to leave the room with these pieces spread out." He looked across the room to where Denise sat flipping through magazines she had read several times. "Would you mind bringing Miss Barbour's jewelry box to me?"

Denise unfolded herself from the couch, return-ing a few moments later with the cheap fake-leather box, its earlier garish pinkness dulled with uneven smudges.

Cort opened it by popping the simple lock and poked through the contents. Suddenly he gasped.

"This proves it!" he proclaimed. "Look at this!" He held a silver pin under the light and stared at

Jean with almost accusatory intensity. "The other rose!"

"What?" Jean asked, blinking her eyes into focus against her fatigue.

"The other rose!"

The pin was indeed a silver bas-relief of a fully opened cabbage rose. It was something she enjoyed wearing on a rather romantic pink silk blouse she had purchased during a flush period a few years ago. She wore it when she wanted to look elegant, in those moments when jeans and T-shirts weren't appropriate.

"So?" Jean asked.

"So!" Cort exclaimed with a grim nod. He turned over the slightly tarnished silver to examine the markings on the back and then glared at Jean. Just as suddenly his expression softened. "Of course you don't know . . ."

When he turned to writing rather than explaining, Jean relaxed in her chair and yawned. It was difficult to remain alert. Even Denise's strong coffee wasn't keeping her eyes open.

Cort studied a silver-and-turquoise pendant and matching earrings of rather nice design and craftsmanship for southwestern Native American jewelry, but not of particular interest to him. He paused in making a sketch of them, more to let his cramped fingers rest than to study either the jewelry or the woman who sat across the table from him.

But what was intended to be a mere glance at Jean became a long appraisal of a lovely woman who was fighting hard to stay awake. Her eyes half-open, half-closed, as though she was afraid she would miss something. The garish light of the overhead fixture created a halo effect around her hair as her head tilted. He wanted to reach out and touch her, just as he had when he had first seen her.

Cort realized he probably could have convinced her to go into the hotel manager's office with him without grabbing her arm, but he hadn't been able to resist that physical contact.

Without taking his eyes off her, Cort reached for the coffee cup beside him and grimaced when he found it empty. José would have refilled it, but Cort signaled him to stay where he was with a shake of his head. Cort looked across the table once more before picking up his pen again.

Certain of his ancestors would have reached for a paintbrush when confronted by such beauty. He, on the other hand, would rather reach for the woman herself.

Shifting in his chair, he felt the weight of his pistol resting against his ribs. Yes, he might have to reach for it if things got nasty before this woman and her incredible possessions were safe.

The next thing Jean knew, a noise had roused her. It was the creaking of Cort's chair as he

41

leaned back. And then she heard the closing of the heavy back door of the deli below as Levi Freeman arrived to start his breads and pastries. They'd been sitting at the table all night, she realized.

"Well, Miss Barbour, you should consider yourself a very fortunate woman," Cort proclaimed. "How you acquired this assortment is a mystery to me, but I am willing to listen to any explanation you give."

Jean blinked again and stretched her back. "What do you mean?"

"These items, plus those in the hotel safe, are worth well over a million dollars, young lady," he informed her, pointing the tip of his pen toward the two-page inventory. "And that is a conservative figure. I suggest they be put in a safe place."

"You're kidding!" Jean exclaimed. "This is some kind of scam. A con game of some sort—"

"No." Cort got to his feet and flexed his shoulders wearily. "I suggest you find more appropriate clothes, and I'll take you to see convincing evidence. Have your roommate watch your jewels while you change."

Hurrying into her bedroom and carefully removing Denise's gown, Jean changed into jeans, tennis shoes, and a tailored shirt and pulled on an Irish knit sweater over the ensemble. She could look as casual as anyone she had ever seen cruising in their yachts or strolling on the palm-shaded beaches.

Cort watched attentively as Jean packed the jewelry into her large purse to take with her, as he insisted. Deep inside she had a doubt, but it was one she wanted to leave in the apartment. She scampered down the steps behind the chauffeur to the limo, standing cold and dew-moistened in the January morning.

Once inside, Jean shivered. Cort stretched an arm behind her to pull her closer to him, but she resisted. She was sitting to his left and was all too aware of the pistol holstered just above his belt.

Sensing the reason for Jean's reluctance, Cort smiled in the dim light of dawn and chuckled softly. Perhaps later, he mused.

Before long the car rolled sedately through wrought-iron gates, past a phalanx of lawn sprinklers that kept the grass an emerald green even during the dry winter. Tall palm trees and a spreading flamboyant tree guarded the drive leading to the porte cochere of a Spanish-style mansion. The crashing of the waves of the Atlantic was a rhythmic counterpoint to the gusting breeze.

Cort's excitement was visibly growing as he grasped Jean's hand and pulled her behind him into the foyer of the house.

He tugged her along to the main salon, where he turned on the light over an oil portrait. "There," he said almost reverently.

A woman peered down at them with a certain hauteur. Around her throat, at her ears, and on her hands were regally-worn diamonds. Almost as an afterthought to all that splendor, at the center of the low neckline of her gown reposed the brooch Jean had worn the night before. There could be no mistaking it.

"Ohh . . ." Jean sighed, understanding part of Cort's excitement.

"So, you recognize it?"

"Yes! But how—" She tore her eyes away from Cort's triumphant face to look again at the skillful artist's rendering of the brooch on the portrait. "How did my great-grandmother get something that was obviously worth a lot of money?"

"That, Miss Barbour, is what we must try to discover. But that's not the only thing I want to show you," Cort told her, his eyes sparkling in the faint light coming into the room from the pink Atlantic dawn.

Then with an abruptness Jean was beginning to notice as habitual, he snapped out the light and struck out for some other part of the huge house.

Glad she had worn soft-soled shoes, Jean hurried to keep up with him. They passed over polished floors through high-ceilinged rooms that she would rather have strolled through leisurely, as she would to fully appreciate a museum.

He pushed though a solid swinging door into a kitchen fitted with gleaming commercial appliances and all manner of utensils hanging from racks and hooks.

"I'm starving." He stopped abruptly in the middle of the deserted room and stared first at the stove and then at the double-doored refrigerator.

"And you don't cook?"

"Very little, and only in my own home," Cort responded. "But I hesitate in someone else's house."

"Perhaps this is the cook's day off," Jean suggested, hearing only the breeze and the waves outside the house when she cocked her head to listen.

"Undoubtedly Piet and Kiki will sleep late," Cort noted disapprovingly. It was clear that he thought if he was up, everyone else should be also. It did not matter that he hadn't had a wink of sleep the night before. He was bright-eyed and ready for another day. How dare the cook not be in the kitchen when he needed something to eat!

"I could whip up something for you," Jean offered. She dropped her purse onto a nearby stool and opened the refrigerator. There was a pitcher of orange juice, a commercial container of pancake or crepe batter, and a bowl of washed strawberries, plump and red, front and center. Obviously the cook did not want to have much to do when she reported later in the morning.

"Aha!" Jean exclaimed, taking the batter and holding it to the light to read the directions. "That looks easy enough to me," she said, handing the container to Cort.

"You can say that," he said with a chuckle. "You read English."

"Don't you?"

"Newspaper and book English, not cooking

45

English."

"What do you speak?" Jean asked, looking around for a skillet or, better yet, a waffle maker.

"As a native? Dutch. Then German, French, Italian, Greek." He ticked off the languages on his long, blunt fingers. "Some Polish, Russian, Danish, Spanish, and a bit of Hebrew. And dialects."

"You must be a quick study," Jean complimented, comparing two skillets she was trying to decide on. She empathized with Cort's reluctance to use a strange kitchen, but her own hunger drove her on.

Just as she was about to search out the cooking oil, there was a stirring at the outside door and a heavyset woman in a light-gray uniform entered the kitchen.

"Huh! Who are you?" she demanded of Jean, removing the shapeless sweater she'd thrown around her shoulders.

"She's with me," Cort came to her defense. "We need something to eat."

The cook surveyed Cort's formal clothes through thick glasses that magnified her red-rimmed eyes, then looked again at Jean with an approving if slightly grudging nod. "Mr. van Roy, you go get out of those fancy duds and I'll have some crepes and strawberries right soon. I suppose you're goin' yachtin' this mornin'. Try to duck this time when the boom swings."

She chuckled heartily to herself, unconcerned about any breach of servant-employer etiquette with Cort van Roy, a sort of guest, one who was a bit strange at that.

"Well, uh . . ." Cort mumbled. He started toward the door they had entered. "Perhaps you'd like to wait in one of the sitting rooms while I change. Mrs. Ghent will probably serve breakfast in the garden room. Maybe there are some magazines . . ."

Jean scooped up her purse and followed him out. "I'll amuse myself," she told him confidently.

Chapter Three

Some noise roused Kiki van Roy from her fitful sleep. Perhaps it was the sound of tires on the brick driveway and the low purr of Cort's car engine, or the closing of the garage door as José put the limo away.

Cort would be coming up the carpeted steps to the second floor any moment now, through the upstairs sitting room, and past the doors to the master suite to the guest room he was using.

She often thought that it would have been interesting to know what might have happened if she had met Pieter's Dutch cousin before she had met her husband. But she knew she could drive herself crazy trying to second-guess fate. Some things could not be changed.

She'd had too much champagne the night before. So had Pieter, for that matter, and she was glad they'd also hired a limo for the night. Pieter would have insisted on driving otherwise. And she would have been scared to death that he would have slammed their vehicle into a palm tree.

Why wasn't Cort van Roy coming up the stairs? What was taking him so long?

She heard the distant, muffled voices below. Far away. Probably in the kitchen. Strange. Mrs. Ghent shouldn't be in yet. And it could not be his man José, whose voice had a low resonance that was unmistakable. It was a light female voice. Cort must have brought someone home with him.

Half the women at the gala would have given their right arm to come home with Cort van Roy. They were only encouraged by his aloofness.

Why on earth did he single out that poorly-disguised mouse in the déclassé gown for his attentions? Granted, she had a certain élan. That was usually sadly lacking in the crowd of gadflies who circulated through the endless round of social functions searching for perspective mates.

Kiki heard the back door grate and realized with certainty that Mrs. Ghent was only now arriving. Cort had indeed brought someone home with him.

Damn! He spent the whole night with that woman and brought her into my home! Of all the nerve!

In all the years Kiki had known Cort, he had never done such a thing. She thought he might die of terminal discretion. That was why Kiki felt safe in fantasizing about him. She was assured that if she let a stray word of her attraction slip, if by some action she betrayed herself, Cort would never take advantage of the situation. Her ten-year marriage to Pieter would never be compromised by Cort.

Pieter lay sleeping beside her, snoring softly from time to time, oblivious to her presence in the king-sized bed. He seemed not to notice her, to take her for granted much too often. No wonder she liked to pretend about the darkly-handsome and elusive Cort van Roy when he made his infrequent and much too short visits to Palm Beach.

She heard footsteps on the stairs — a single set of footsteps, not lagging from exhaustion but firm and full of purpose, exasperatingly normal. Then there was the closing of the guest room door, followed almost predictably by the sluicing sound of the shower. Kiki could visualize the stream of steamy water hitting Cort's firm flesh.

Abruptly she bolted from her bed, making the uneasy dull ache in her forehead surge momentarily. She groped for the back of the vanity chair and lowered herself to the padded seat, afraid to look at her reflection in the mirror.

She had to stop thinking these thoughts! She was married to Pieter. And without marriage she was nothing.

Obviously there was someone in the house whom Cort wanted present. Whoever it was ought to at least be acknowledged, even if it was that impossible creature Cort had been with at Casino Night. She would have to make herself presentable and put in an appearance.

Coffee. She needed coffee, Kiki thought, pressing her fingertips to her forehead.

A few minutes later she entered the garden room, expecting Mrs. Ghent to be there, setting places for breakfast. Instead, she saw a woman dressed in a sweater and jeans, staring out at the sea.

When the woman turned, Kiki stiffened. Her worst fears had been realized. It was the blonde from the party the night before. The most disturbing thing about her presence, aside from jeans that were nearly white at the knees and the beautifully-handknit sweater that was slightly older than Kiki would have deigned to wear, was that the stranger seemed perfectly at ease, as though she belonged here.

Jean faced Kiki van Roy across the garden room. With its hanging plants and wicker furniture, the room formed a graceful transition from the wild Atlantic shore beyond the windows to the plush formality of the mansion within. It all seemed to be designed to enhance the scale and coloring of Kiki, who stood surveying Jean from head to toe.

Jean decided not to be intimidated by the elegant lady of the house. What if the marabou-trimmed wrapper and pink satin mules cost her husband more than Jean could justify spending on her entire wardrobe? That didn't make Kiki any better under the skin than Jean was.

Kiki was not, after all, so much older than Jean that she should be off-putting. What could she be? Five, maybe seven, years older? She'd probably married Pieter van Roy right out of some fancy New England women's college. Oh, yes, you learned a lot from the *Shiny Sheet* if you read between the lines. There was a certain track the elite followed through life, and few could stray from it without dire social consequences.

"Good morning," Jean greeted her, with a cheerful but firm voice.

Kiki van Roy made a sound that was close to an impolite grunt, and Jean knew what she was thinking.

Kiki looked around for something, but the table had not yet been set for breakfast, and there was no sign or scent of the morning meal. "I'll see what is keeping Mrs. Ghent from serving," Kiki mumbled and stalked off to the kitchen.

Jean had the satisfaction of knowing in her heart that Kiki was having uncomfortable and erroneous thoughts of what had happened between her and Cort van Roy.

Jean returned her attention to the ocean,

watching the gulls take their breakfast from the roiling surf. It was not quite the comfort that Jean had hoped.

Cort was an extremely attractive man. The moments they had spent together led Jean to believe that he did not put her in the same class with, say, one of the dead fish on the beach. But she knew her place, for once.

So this is what Great-grandmother Finney had been exposed to at one time, Jean thought, running her hand over the back of a chair.

Somehow that magnificent brooch had changed hands from the van Roys to a servant — the servant of another family. If she could just piece it all together in some logical order, maybe she could disprove the suspicions she saw in Cort's beautiful eyes.

The sum of what she knew of Great-gramma Finney's youth uncoiled from her memory. In February 1925 the seventeen-year-old maid could well have been in Palm Beach.

It was well-known back home that the McClellans, the oil-wealthy family Delia Baker worked for, had their own railroad car to take them to Florida every winter and Maine every summer. Jean had often heard the story of how a selected few servants were taken along, generally to take care of elderly Mrs. McClellan and the wardrobe of the younger women. Mr. McClellan's wife, Beatrice, and Miss Helene McClellan, a young woman of marriageable age, would also make the trips. Aha! Perhaps that had something to do with it.

Jean glanced around the room and up at the detail where the walls met the ceiling. If there were only some way to get these walls to talk. Perhaps they could tell the story, to clear the air of the suspicion that drifting like a cloud around Jean now.

She didn't want to think that anyone in her lineal background had done something—well, shady. She had inherited a sort of pride about her relatives. Perhaps she'd been carrying the epithet "poor but honest" like an unseen family motto on a crest of the symbols of toil and perseverance. That her great-grandmother would have—could have—stolen a gem of such obvious worth was unthinkable.

All that Jean could remember of the family history of that time was that Delia Baker had married Tom Finney in the summer of 1925. She had left the McClellans's home to work with her husband for some people with a large farm in the next county. A few years later Tom opened a mechanic's garage in town and Delia worked as a day-lady for families who no longer hired full-time, live-in help.

Years later, the widowed Delia took positions as practical nurse for aging women who could no longer care for themselves. It seemed like honest work, all of it, and she would not have been employed by the best families in town if she hadn't been a pillar of respectability.

A noise behind Jean interrupted her troubled reverie. Mrs. Ghent, stiffly officious, wheeled a tea cart into the garden room and began setting the table for four. From the expression on her lined face, she appeared to be angry. Perhaps this was not a job she acknowledged as hers as cook, or perhaps Kiki had not been very diplomatic about how promptly she expected breakfast.

Jean smiled uncertainly and was rewarded with only a nod from the old woman.

When Mrs. Ghent returned to the kitchen, Jean was puzzled by the woman's obvious age. She had to be older than retirement age. She had to be in her seventies, at least. And getting up on Sunday morning to prepare breakfast for someone as unappreciative as Kiki van Roy! No wonder she was out of sorts.

Carrying a Sunday paper, Kiki appeared at the same time that Mrs. Ghent brought an urn of coffee into the room and placed it on a sideboard between a riotously blooming white azalea and a pitcher of orange juice.

After pouring herself a cup of coffee, Kiki settled into one of the white wicker chairs at the table and proceeded to ignore Jean while she sorted sections of the Sunday paper.

Jean was amused to see that she opened the society section first, something Jean read only when Denise brought it to her attention.

With barely a sound from his deck shoes, Cort entered the room, nonchalantly gorgeous in white pants and a navy knit shirt, his hair still damp from his shower. A white cable-knit sweater hung limply from his hand, pointing up the contrast between its soft whiteness and the tanned muscularity of his strong forearm.

"Good morning, Kiki!" he greeted his cousin's wife, his eyes registering surprise that his cousin's wife was up at that hour. "You do remember Jean from last night, don't you?"

Kiki composed her face into an insincerely polite smile, as though he'd entered during a temporary lull in what had been a spirited gabble of girl-talk.

"Ah, good!" Cort sighed, not letting on whether he had seen through Kiki. He picked up two of the cups that had been at the unoccupied places at the table and proceeded to fill them from the urn.

After he returned the cups to their places, he pulled both chairs out and made it clear to Jean that she was to sit down.

Jean couldn't remember the last time a man had held a chair for her. She might have been confused by the attention if she hadn't been amused by Kiki's animosity.

"Could I borrow the boat this morning?" Cort asked Kiki as his long, tanned fingers unfolded the white linen napkin at his place and draped it over his lap.

"Oh, go ahead!" Kiki said peevishly, rustling her paper. "Piet won't want it until this afternoon, if at all. We didn't get in until two this morning, and he's still sleeping."

"Ah, we'll have it to ourselves, then," Cort exclaimed, flashing a look toward Jean. "Have you ever sailed?"

Jean shook her head, probably sliding a few more notches in Kiki's esteem, but she refused to lie.

"There's nothing like it," Cort told her enthusiastically. "Out on the water, no one around to bother you, to hear what you say or see what you do. It's the only privacy left, I think."

The secret message he was giving her was just as obviously misinterpreted by Kiki, who settled her jaw and snapped the newspaper in her hands once more as she ducked behind it.

Luckily it was at that moment that Mrs. Ghent served the strawberry crepes.

Kiki put her paper aside and turned her attention to her breakfast, shooting occasional dagger glances toward Jean.

When Cort noticed the rather one-sided battle, his long eyelashes flickered once over his gray-gold eyes and his lips curved in a gentle, knowing smile.

"Perhaps we can stay out on the water longer than just a few hours," Cort said lazily, almost as a question.

"That would be nice," Jean mumbled inanely,

but it obviously satisfied Cort. He looked quickly at Kiki, who was doing a slow burn.

So that's how it is between them! Jean thought, cutting into the wafer-thin crepe with the edge of her fork.

Cort observed every nuance of Kiki's snobbish possessiveness and was not above turning it against her. He was a deceptively-docile opponent, but he had a sense of humor after all.

Jean smiled back at him with new respect.

Putting off their sail for a few minutes, Cort led Jean into a book-lined library and searched the shelves for a photograph album among the score or so that filled one shelf.

"You'll recognize another piece of jewelry here," he told her, opening the book almost to the page he wanted on the first try. "This is the mother of Ruta van Roy, the woman who was wearing your diamond brooch."

Jean's eyes widened as she followed the manicured tip of his finger to the woman's Gibson-style bodice. There was the silver cabbage rose, one of several brooches pinned to her dress.

"Good heavens!" Jean gasped, sitting down at the table where Cort had spread the album. "How do you suppose my great-grandmother got that?"

Cort shrugged. "Do you recognize anything else?"

Jean studied the picture minutely, even using the small magnifying glass Cort handed her. "No . . . no," she said, sighing, after studying the photograph. "Some of those pieces must have been very beautiful, but I don't recognize them."

"It's just as well." Cort sat down beside her and rested his chin on his hand. He seemed content just to watch her for a moment.

Jean wrenched her attention away from the sensual lines of his mouth to look back at the album. She turned the pages until she reached the last of the pictures, then went forward of the photograph that established the early existence of the silver rose.

A fearsome-looking man with an elaborate beard and mustache glared out at her. He was dressed in dated formal wear, his chest draped with a broad sash, replete with jeweled medals. On the next page was a companion piece, a woman of regal bearing, a sparkling tiara nestled in her gray curls, her gown also sashed and bearing some sort of medal.

Jean's mind reeled, not consciously assessing what she was seeing. She went on to other pages, walling away the thought that struggled to form.

"Impressive," Jean complimented at last, looking up from the book.

A flicker of humor crossed Cort's face. "A lot has changed over the years since those pictures were taken." He leaned forward in his chair, suddenly serious. "I can't understand how you came to possess either of the pieces, but I believe you are the rightful owner. Somehow I cannot find a reason to suspect you of a robbery that took place long before you were born, if indeed it actually happened."

"Thank you," Jean said, closing the book carefully, if reluctantly. She loved looking at old pictures, even of people she had little interest in.

Cort slowly got to his feet and scanned the room. Over the marble mantel hung a lovely landscape in oil. He crossed to it and ran his fingers under the frame, then shook his head. Nearby there was another picture, a small Dutch portrait. Again he traced the edge of the frame and then smiled.

"The safe," he explained. "Your purse, Jean. If we're leaving the house, we must put everything in a secure place."

"Oh?" Jean asked, then reached for the leather bag and removed her jewelry from it. "Yes, I guess that's wise."

She was amazed that Cort opened the wall vault by listening to the tumblers of the lock. "I really don't think I should trust you," she teased, almost unable to keep from giggling.

"Oh, this was too easy. I'll tell Piet to get something more sophisticated." He closed the metal door on Jean's jewelry and replaced the picture, wiping the frame with his handkerchief. "I hope Mrs. Ghent has our picnic ready."

* * *

Jean's sneakered foot touched the deck of the van Roy yacht, the *Merry Weather,* with more trepidation than she had felt in a long time. "I'm reminded of the old Irish prayer that ends, 'The sea is so big and my boat is so small.' "

"One must respect the sea," Cort agreed, letting go of her hand to put the picnic hamper in the galley.

"I warned you," she reminded him, securing her hair with a bandanna she had tucked into her pocket, "I know nothing about sailing."

"Then just do as I say," Cort called back, his voice muted slightly by the breeze.

"That's what I'm afraid of." Jean laughed.

"We'll use the motor," he explained, "at least to get away from the dock. After all, the object is to get out onto the water so that we can talk, not to teach you a short course in sailing."

"I'm glad you understand that," Jean told him, looking up at him as he emerged from the hatch. He'd put his sweater on, and she admired how it stretched across his muscular chest.

A serene smile lighting his eyes, Cort proceeded to cast off and do everything himself, seeming to have decided that Jean was a useless passenger.

Actually she decided that she would have liked to learn how to let out the sails and take the helm. Watching Cort move about, lightfooted

61

and sure as a cat, was an amusement in itself. But Jean had learned that it was more fun to jump into whatever experience presented itself and get a few blisters, scrapes, and bruises, than to watch someone else do all the work and have all the fun.

The late-morning ocean was rolling gently under the prow of the sleek white yacht as they caught the breeze and headed for open water.

Jean sat on the padded lid of a locker close to the helm and unashamedly watched Cort handle the wheel. At last he turned the boat into the wind and scampered across the deck to lower the sails. The boat stopped moving forward and bobbed on the swells, barely in sight of land.

"You really like this, don't you?" Jean asked as she watched him scan the horizon, his sturdy legs braced against the motion of the boat.

"Yes!" he answered emphatically and grinned. "Every year I try to come while Pieter is here so we can sail and pretend we are kids again."

Jean squinted up into the clear light that glinted off the waves. "Were you children together?"

"Not children. Teenagers. You have to understand the van Roy family," Cort explained, going back to the helm and making a minor correction. "Pieter is from a part of the family that got trapped in the States during World War II and stayed here. My part of the family went into exile in England. Anyway, when Pieter and I were teens, we were sent to the same military prep school in Connecticut because my father was posted to a very sensitive if unattractive post of the diplomatic service of the Netherlands. I thought it was wonderful to be accepted into the life of the prep school as a friend and relative of Pieter's."

"So that's why your English is fluent," Jean observed.

"Pieter taught me to speak English slang like a native," he said, his eyes reflecting happy thoughts of his youth. "Unfortunately, he was good enough at Dutch to translate textbook English for me so that my reading of formal English never got terribly good, and since I don't get much practice at it now, I'm not great at it. I can read newspapers and letters easily enough, but reading a novel in English is not a choice I make often."

"Did you both go into the Navy?"

Cort shook his head. "We weren't required to by the terms of our school. Pieter went on to Harvard, and I went back to the Netherlands. But by then Father was posted to Spain, so I split the difference and went to the University of Paris."

"The Sorbonne?" Jean asked. "What did you study?"

Cort's mouth curved into a smile, and he sat down on the locker beside her. "French women," he replied flippantly, then became serious. "No,

I studied everything I could observe. But it seemed that the old family interests kept pushing me into what I am doing now. We have been interested in jewels for generations, and art for even longer. One thing led to another, and I was asked to join Interpol for my expert knowledge in identifying artwork and gems."

"Is it exciting, or just . . . a job?"

"A bit of each," Cort responded. He seemed to take one last long look at the sea, then brought his eyes to rest on Jean.

"Now we can talk." He sprawled on the locker with her, leaning his shoulders against the bulkhead and squinting at her against the sun. "First of all, you must take better care of all the lovely pieces of jewelry you own. They are dirty, getting scratched from coming in contact with each other. Such a shame." He shook his head sadly.

"What can I do?" Jean asked, taking his criticism much too personally. "No one ever told me—"

Cort waved his hand to dismiss her objections. "What has happened in the past is not important at the moment. You can remedy that easily enough by buying a nice velvet-lined jewelry box for your collection, then renting a safety-deposit box at a bank for the most valuable pieces. But tell me, have you given any thought to how your great-grandmother got the roses in the first place?"

"The roses?"

He shrugged. "That's how I think of them. The silver piece is obvious. The diamond is a double rose cut, and the setting is intended to be a rose."

Jean nodded at his somewhat romantic logic, finding it oddly touching. "I thought of it more as a tulip," she mused. "And there's no way it can be worn upright, the way a flower would grow. Believe me, I've tried it a hundred times over the years."

"That's because it was designed to be worn precisely the way you wore it last night, with the blossom downward," Cort pointed out. "It's a lovely little story. You see, before roses were hybridized — right? — they wilted very soon after being cut. Hence the saying that the rose paled in comparison to the wearer. So as magnificent as the van Roy stone is, it pales, it wilts, in comparison to . . . to you, its owner."

Jean laughed at the flattery. "Oh, somewhere you are Irish, m'lad!"

Suddenly Cort laughed, throwing his head back and letting the deep, rich sound float above them, joining them in more comfortable companionship. Cort turned to her once again.

"Now, tell me about your great-grandmother," he urged.

"Great-gramma Finney could very well have been in Palm Beach in February 1925." Jean sighed. "Don't you just wish you could go back in time and find out how it happened?"

"Might there be someone in your family who could tell you what happened?" Cort asked, nonchalantly stretching his arm along the rail behind Jean.

"As far as I know, everyone is gone," Jean told him. "My mother died five years ago, and she wasn't one to gossip. My grandmother Grant used to tell me stories, but I can't remember them. Some of them were too outlandish—at least, it seemed that way to me. She was the one who used to let me play with the diamond brooch."

"Then what did she say about it?" Cort asked.

Admitting that she didn't remember would do no good, she knew. "I'll try to remember," she promised him, but after searching her mind for a few minutes, she shook her head.

"What about the other things you have—the silver-and-crystal necklace with the little diamond . . ."

"That was a gift from my grandfather to my grandmother before they even got engaged," Jean said, glad that she had a ready answer. "On my father's side. That was in the late twenties."

Cort's eyebrow raised. "At a time when diamonds were devalued," he said thoughtfully.

"I have a bracelet that goes with it, but I left it at home because the clasp wasn't secure. I suppose my stepmother has it now."

"It might help to go back to your home and see what is there," Cort suggested. "There just might be someone who can tell you the story—"

"I don't want to go home," Jean told him, smiling indulgently. "It's January, for heaven's sake! It gets cold up there. They have snow and ice and—yech! That's why I'm here."

"Where is your home?" Cort asked.

"Oil City, Pennsylvania."

"Where's that?"

Jean sighed. "I'll show you on a map when we get back to shore. Anyway, I'm not about to pick up and go there when the weather up there is bad."

Cort was silent for a long moment, surveying the sea with narrowed eyes. "Jean, my dear, there is a pair of binoculars just inside the hatch. Could you please hand them to me?"

"Sure," Jean agreed, not thinking it strange that he asked the favor because she was just a few steps from the hatch. When she handed the case to him, he unsnapped it and handed the binoculars to her.

"Why did you ask me to get them if you—"

"Can you see a boat on the horizon?"

"Barely," Jean answered, then lifted the glasses to her eyes. "Wow, these are powerful."

"Keep your eyes on that boat for a moment for me, love." He was shifting on the locker beside her, and she wondered what he was doing. Taking her eyes briefly from the glasses, she noticed he was checking to see that the pistol he carried was loaded.

"My God, Cort!" she gasped. "What the—"

"Just to be on the safe side," he said evenly, tucking the gun into the back waistband of his slacks and tugging his sweater down over the grip. "Have you seen any identification on the boat?"

"I can read the *Sugar Daddy*."

"All right, Jean, what I am going to ask you to do is probably going to make very little sense to you, but just be very patient with me, play along, and make it look convincing," Cort said, moving the binoculars aside. His arms closed around her slowly and deliberately, and his mouth touched hers, barely any pressure at first.

"Convincing . . ." he repeated huskily, intimately, as though whoever was out there on the water could hear them.

Yes, she needed to be reminded it was an act for some strange purpose she could not guess at. It was not difficult to run her hand over the soft bulkiness of his sweater at his powerful shoulders, or to delve her fingers into the black silkiness of his hair as he turned his back to the oncoming boat.

The *Merry Weather* pitched as it rode a swell, and Jean tightened the arm that she had at first placed gently at his waist. As the vessel lurched, something inside her had a similar reaction and all thoughts of faking a response left her mind.

Cort sighed and let her go just long enough to turn them around so that he could glimpse the boat without being obvious.

"Do you think they're watching us?" she asked, looking closely at his gray-gold eyes, especially at the discolored one.

"Undoubtedly, they are," Cort answered. "I must assume that my adversaries know Piet's boat and that I borrow it every chance I get. I only hope they have not slipped some sort of listening device aboard. Now, my dear, let us move slowly inside. I want you to be out of harm's way."

Jean didn't know just how far out of harm's way she would be on this yacht, which probably had a number of bunks. It was not something she wanted to think about. And she needn't have worried about it for an instant. Once they were concealed by the hatch, Cort snatched the binoculars from her and searched the horizon from behind a loosely-woven drape at a porthole.

"Now what?" Jean asked nervously.

"They're bearing off," Cort told her, calm relief in his voice. "They're heading south. So let's wait for them to be out of earshot and we'll circle north and back to shore."

"Why?"

"Because I don't trust them not to run out and come back at us from another angle."

"Who, Cort? Please tell me."

Cort turned from the porthole and pointed to his puffy left eye. "Someone who does not like me, on a professional level."

"A jewel thief? The man from last night. De-Pesca?"

"You're very quick, very . . . attentive," Cort said appreciatively.

He snapped the binoculars back into the case and hung them on the hook where she had gotten them. "We have work to do, Jean," he told her, taking the ladder rungs two at a time to the deck and taking over the helm.

The motor growled to life. He swung the boat in a wide arc and headed back to shore.

Jean studied the grim set of his jaw and his narrowed eyes as he surveyed the horizon. Whoever else might have been convinced by their on-deck charade, she wasn't. His kiss was in the line of duty; his charm was turned on and off when it was in his best interests.

She wondered why she cared so much, why she had wanted him to convince her of affection he probably did not feel.

Jean decided that she didn't really like sailing. The water was deep and surly-looking, the wind oppressive, and the other inhabitants of the waves menacing. No, this was not an experience she would embellish for Denise's amusement when she got home. Rich people could have their boats and yachts; Jean would be just as happy staying on shore, skipping the occasional stone into the surf, and collecting seashells and gull's feathers.

When they were nearing the shore, Jean took

the opportunity to settle something that had bothered her since they had gone to her apartment the night before.

"May I ask you something?"

"Surely," Cort responded, not taking his eyes from their course.

"Did I commit a gaffe last night, inviting your man into the apartment with us and serving him coffee?"

"Why did you think that?"

"Denise told me—"

"Hospitality is never a gaffe," Cort assured her, with a brief flicker of his gray-gold eyes in her direction. "In an orderly world, he might have been safely left by the car, but last night was not . . . safe. I needed him with me, and you made us both very comfortable. If I had not thanked you for that before, I thank you now."

"Is he Interpol, too?"

"In a way."

"What do you mean by that?"

"He's in my employ, but he's cleared by Interpol to assist me when I need him."

"He's not just a servant, a chauffeur, or a valet?"

"No. He's more of a bodyguard."

Jean studied him for a moment, then asked in a lowered voice, "Was he armed?"

Cort nodded.

Stunned into silence, Jean moved away from him.

His mind clearly on his navigating, Cort was almost taciturn while he piloted the *Merry Weather* to the van Roy dock and eased the yacht to her slip.

The entire excursion was a disappointment as far as Jean was concerned. First the lecture, then the play-acting, and now the distant attitude. No, this was definitely not one of the memories to trot out for Denise's entertainment.

Ever the gentleman, Cort took her hand and helped her from the boat onto the dock, making certain that she got her land legs back before they headed to the house.

Cort seemed surprised to see his cousin in swim trunks and terry robe, sunning himself in a lawn chair on the patio beside the pool.

"Why are you back so soon?" Pieter van Roy queried, raising his eyes from the financial section of the newspaper, which he was studying in the lee of a bougainvillea-covered trellis.

"To avoid ambush," Cort growled.

"Your friends of last week?" Pieter asked, a frown creasing his broad forehead. "Humph! And who is this?"

"Jean. I met her at the party last night."

"Oh, yes!" Pieter said, trying to hide any interest he had. Word of Jean's presence must have spread to him very quickly. He rose partially and extended a hand toward her.

Jean really didn't want to shake hands with him, but she did, finding his hand surprisingly calloused but without cordiality.

Cort held the back of one of the expensive patio chairs for her, so she sat down and tried to look at ease and in control, neither of which she was.

"What do you remember, Piet," Cort prodded, sitting down beside her, "of the van Roy roses?"

"Don't ask me to think, Cort!" Pieter pleaded, pinching his gray eyes closed. "I'm hung over and it's all I can do to read."

A wry smile played unevenly across Cort's mouth, affecting the right side of his mouth a bit more than the left. "Failing that, can I borrow your plane?"

"Now? Today?"

"Yes."

"Where do you want to go?" Pieter asked, folding the paper and wedging it between two potted geraniums to keep it from blowing away.

Cort looked at Jean.

"Pennsylvania?" Jean supplied.

Pieter asked, "Philadelphia? Harrisburg?"

"In the western part of the state, the nearest airport is outside Franklin," Jean told him.

Pieter gave her a look that told her either he had never heard of it or, if he had, didn't think much of it.

"You can check my guide to airports in the family room, to see if there will be jet fuel available at a small airport like that," Pieter cautioned, pulling his robe closer around his broad shoulders. "You might refuel somewhere else."

"Jet?" Jean repeated, looking from one to the other.

Cort stroked his chin, then glanced at his watch. "An hour to get ready, three hours to get there. We ought to be there by dark."

"Be where?"

"Wherever it is you are from," Cort said, as though she was an untutored child.

"Oil City?" Jean asked, then shook her head. "No. You don't want to go there. Not this time of year. It's cold. There's ice and snow. Since I've been in Florida, I've realized snow is meant to be seen and not felt."

"Weather." Cort's face took on a distant look, then he got to his feet and turned toward the house. Long strides took him inside without so much as an excuse being tossed over his shoulder. If Pieter was annoyed by his breach of etiquette, he didn't let on.

Cort returned moments later with a more sullen look than Jean had seen before. "I called the weather service and they told me a cold front is moving through that area with blizzards and high winds. It's not advisable to fly in there. The airport will probably be shut down later today."

Jean leaned back in her chair and felt a relaxation of the muscles that had been tense since Cort had mentioned going back to Pennsylvania.

"What now?" she ventured.

"What now, indeed," Cort mused sullenly, slouching in his chair. "By the way, Piet, your safe is woefully obsolete. I opened it in about forty seconds. You must do something about it."

Pieter scowled back at his cousin. "If you say so," he said, getting to his feet and collecting a damp towel from the back of his chair. He took a swat at Cort as he passed him on his way into the house, and Cort grabbed the end of the towel.

A look of camaraderie passed between them, and Pieter entered the house laughing. But the smile on Cort's face faded quickly as he continued to work on a solution to his problem.

Chapter Four

Cort sat at the patio table, drumming his fingers on the tempered glass top as he stared out at the azure water. He had been sitting there for a long time, allowing the sun to wash over the planes of his strong-featured face, the wind to play with the dark strands of his hair.

Abruptly he reached out to pick up the splint picnic basket he had brought from the boat and placed on the flagstones of the patio. He got to his feet decisively and took Jean's hand in his.

"No reason to waste Mrs. Ghent's cooking," he said to Jean as he pulled her up from her chair, his mouth twisting wryly. "Where would you like to eat it?"

Jean looked around, unable to find an inappropriate spot for their lunch. Cort seemed to be drifting across the broad lawn, away from the tables around the patio, past the walkway that led to the tennis court with its cement benches, toward the water again. She followed him, amused by the loose gait of his walk, as though he hadn't a care in the world.

They sat on top of the concrete seawall, dangling their legs over the side above the lapping waves, the lavishly-prepared basket between them.

"Mrs. Ghent knows to pack simple picnics for me," Cort said, lifting neatly-wrapped delicacies from the basket and dividing them between them before moving the basket aside to the grass, not too far away. "None of the chicken salad sandwiches and brie she packs for Kiki and Pieter."

Mrs. Ghent had packed rolls and cheese and slices of a sausage that smelled a bit stronger than Jean thought she could handle at the moment.

Cort combined bits and pieces on his roll and ate with great delight if not speed. He seemed to be enjoying every bite and urged Jean to help herself until finally she shrugged and followed his example.

"We have a picnic park at home," Jean reminisced. "It has lots of tables and play apparatus spread all through the place, not just in a playground. I've never seen anything quite like it in all the places I've been."

"Oh, this is the way to eat when you travel in Europe," Cort explained. "A pastry from a bakery and coffee at a sidewalk café for breakfast, a picnic for lunch, dinner in a neighborhood restaurant in the evening! Have you ever been to Europe?"

Jean shook her head. "I'm having a hard enough time just paying rent and putting food on my table. There's no extra money for a trip to Europe."

"You could sell a piece of your jewelry."

"Oh, sure!" Jean exclaimed. "Now the pitch!"

"Listen! You could sell . . . the opal ring. That would cover airfare. And I would show you France for a week, maybe two. You could stay in my apartment. It wouldn't cost you anything but your airfare."

Jean laughed. "And you have some land to sell me? I might be from a small town, but I came out of the woods a long time ago."

"It is something to think about, Jean," Cort told her, turning back to the picnic basket to find something more to eat. "In jewelry, you are a wealthy woman. You ought to think about enjoying your resources."

There were several large perfect apples, golden pears, and clusters of grapes they eventually fought over.

Jean tore the last of the rolls into crumbs, which she tossed one by one to the circling gulls until, laughing, Cort snatched them all from her hand and tossed them into the air above the water in one grand finale.

Then he stowed wrappers and napkins neatly away and closed the basket.

"No wine?" Jean asked, teasing.

"The boat has its own cellar." Cort shrugged. "I could get some." He pulled his legs up and was about to get to his feet when Jean stopped him with a hand on his arm.

"I had more than enough last night," Jean laughed with a shake of her head.

"So did I," he murmured softly, reaching out to touch a few strands of her long blond ponytail that the wind blew toward him. He wrapped the strands around his fingers and pressed his lips to them, not taking his eyes from hers.

Jean kept herself from giggling by supreme effort. The gesture was endearing, but she was not prepared for the flood of emotion that threatened to overtake her. She had never encountered a European man, nor any man who was obviously so at ease in the wealth and privilege around him. He hadn't seemed the least bit uncomfortable in her apartment the night before, either, and she wondered just where he fit into the world.

The uneasiness she felt had nothing to do with social position. It had to do with feelings that went much deeper, that were much more personal, much more elemental.

"Cort—" she sighed.

"I like the way you say that," he told her, his gray-gold eyes teasing as he let go of her hair by fanning his fingers and letting the breeze carry the pale strands out of his palm.

"I don't understand you."

"Well, I do have some trouble with what and when and where," he reflected. "I didn't think I was doing so badly."

"That's not what I mean."

"What is there to understand when a man meets a woman who—" Cort dropped the sentence and stared out at the sea. "I see what you mean. English is a difficult language to make love in, and with your reluctance to rely on languages foreign to you—"

"It's not reluctance," Jean told him. "It's inability. I had Latin in high school and German in college, neither of which is a bit of help at the moment. The fact remains, we just met."

"We spent the night together," he teased.

Jean frowned. "Cort—"

"I understand now," he said. "Believe me, I come from a strong moral background. I just didn't think American women still had . . . such high standards."

"It might just be the company you keep," Jean pointed out, and was immediately sorry.

"You mean Kiki?" He shifted his legs so that they were no longer hanging over the side of the sea wall but in a lotus position.

"Yes."

"She is unhappy." He shrugged. "It's not my fault. I would never do something to hurt my own family, no matter what I feel. Was that right? What?"

80

Jean nodded. "But people are gossiping about you and Kiki. And I felt her hatred."

"Think nothing of it."

"Then I must mean very little to you. A pretty face you met at a party . . . a woman with a pretty bauble that you are curious about . . . nothing more."

"How can you say that!" He turned toward her and put his hand on her shoulder. "Frankly, I don't know when you fit into my life. Where you fit into my life," he corrected himself, "but you must."

"I must?" Jean raised her eyebrows. "You like to give orders, Cort, but I don't like to take them. I have no idea what you are doing, whether you're who you say you are or a con man with a very believable line. I certainly don't feel comfortable with your cousin and his wife, so unless you have some really good reason for me to stay here one more minute, you'd better come up with it, or I'm out of here."

He drew his legs up, then stretched them out on the grassy lawn behind her. Before she could fully comprehend what was happening, he was kissing her, first on the side of her neck, then her cheek and temple.

The tense restraint of his actions, so slow, so deliberate, so hypnotizing, drove any thought of retreat from Jean's mind.

"American women are always in such a hurry," Cort lamented. "They have no appreciation of courtship as an art form. They want instant gratification and instant commitment! Can't you let destiny work things out for us, even for a moment?"

"Can't you see me as an individual?" she asked. "I'm not like . . ."

"Kiki? Good! Then I'll have to study you closely to see how you are different. It's true that you are not like the idle rich women I have met here, because you did not know how valuable is something you own. I like that. You have character and—What is the word I want? Whimsy! I like that."

More than the wind off the rolling Atlantic Ocean caused the gooseflesh that Jean felt prickle under her heavy Irish sweater. And more than the midday sun caused the blush that colored her cheeks.

She drew her knees up and wrapped her arms around them, wondering why she was taking such a defensive posture. Part of her believed him, the other part didn't. It was like watching a snake, appreciating its beauty yet fearing its venom, and being already paralyzed, unable to react.

"Your eyes start fires in my soul," Cort told her. "I just get them all put out when you look at me again, and I am helpless."

Jean was casting about for a response when she heard footsteps on the lawn behind them.

"Sir! Telephone call for Miss Barbour," a

maid called from a discreet distance.

"Who knows I'm here?" Jean asked, getting to her feet.

"Your roommate. I gave her the number," Cort said, picking up the picnic basket and handing it to the maid as they hurried to the house.

Cort shook his head when Jean would have picked up the cordless telephone that was lying on the patio table.

"That's not secure," he hissed, pulling her along to the phone in the garden room.

When she picked it up, he clasped her wrist and made her hold the receiver slightly away from her ear so that he, too, could hear the conversation.

"Denise? What's wrong?" Jean asked.

"In the vernacular, our apartment has been tossed," Denise answered, her voice barely controlled.

"Are you all right?" Jean asked, grasping the edge of the credenza to support herself.

"Yes. I'm down in the deli. I've called the police, but they aren't here yet."

"Stay right there. We're on our way." When she turned to Cort, he was already telling the maid to have his driver bring his car from the garage.

"Damn," he muttered, taking Jean's arm. "Can you hear anything wrong in her voice? Is she all right?"

"Yes," she assured him. "She's street-smart,

much tougher than I am. She'll be fine in a little while."

When they reached the street where the Freeman Deli stood, there was a police car at the curb, and behind it was another car of the same make and model. Cort paid particular attention to the configuration of antennae on the second sedan and looked pleased with what he saw.

Her dark-brown hair even more disheveled than usual, Denise was sitting at a window table in the deli, a mug of coffee clutched in her tense hands, anxiously staring out the window when Jean and Cort entered.

"Tell me what happened," Jean demanded, sitting down on a chair beside Denise and wrapping her arm around her shaken roommate's shoulders.

"After you left, I straightened the apartment," Denise said, her piercing dark eyes anxious. "I hung the dress you wore last night on the door of my closet, then took the laundry over to the laundromat. When I came back, I came in here for a danish and coffee before I tackled the floors. I was sitting right here when I heard footsteps up in my bedroom. At first I thought you were back, but we rarely go into each other's rooms, especially if the other one isn't there," she explained one of their standing rules for Cort's benefit. "Besides, I knew you had

84

sneakers on, and it sounded like someone heavier. So I told Joey there was someone up there and I was going to see who it was." She took another gulp of her coffee.

"And I told her she should stay put," Levi Freeman's skinny grandson Joey contributed as he came to the table with two mugs and placed them in front of Jean and Cort, then stayed to hear Denise recount her story.

A uniformed police officer and a detective strolled in from the back entrance of the deli and lounged nearby.

"So I went up the steps really carefully, and I heard more moving around in there, drawers opening and closing, and I knew it couldn't be you. I went to the end of the hall and hid in the broom closet until the man came out. It was only about two minutes, but it seemed like two hours."

"Did you get a good look at him?" the detective asked, pen poised over his notebook.

"Not of his face," Denise complained. "But he was wearing jeans and a gray sweatshirt, probably trying to blend in with this neighborhood. Except that the jeans were too new and his shoes were shiny black oxfords, not work shoes or running shoes. He used surgical gloves, and he wiped the doorknob with his handkerchief."

"Not much to go on—" the detective said dubiously.

"Wait," Denise interrupted, always the astute

observer of what people wore and how they acted. "He was probably in his late thirties. He had the walk of someone who was naturally agile, but from the rolls over his belt, he looked a little past his prime—"

"Simon!" Cort exclaimed, brightening with recognition, and the detective nodded. "Why the hell isn't he still in jail?" he demanded of the detective.

"He was never in jail," the detective explained. "We couldn't charge him with trespassing because he never came into the hotel last night. And DePesca walked about four o'clock this morning."

"Is that who was in the boat?" Jean asked.

"Yes," Cort told her. "Simon must have followed us last night even though José thought he didn't. It's hard to hide a limousine, eh? Denise, were you playing your radio this morning?"

"Yes, I turned it on before you and Jean left and turned it off when I went to the laundromat." She hit her forehead with her hand. "That's how he knew someone was in the apartment and then that it was empty. God!"

"You're coming over to the place where I'm staying," Cort stated firmly, getting to his feet. "Both of you. Go pack enough for two days."

"Be prepared to tell us if anything is missing," the detective warned when they started up the steps to the apartment. "We may need a list."

Denise and Jean entered the apartment cautiously, trying to determine what, if anything, was missing, but it was apparent some things were merely moved slightly.

"I'd rather go to my aunt's," Denise groused as she threw clothes into the faded blue duffel bag on her bed.

"I'd feel better if we were together," Jean told her.

"No. I need to be with family."

"I'll arrange a police escort for you," Cort offered. "I want to be sure you're not followed."

"Where Tia Consuela lives, not even your jewel thieves would go," Denise informed him with a touch of irony in her voice.

"Then why are you going there?" he asked.

"I'll be safe," Denise assured him. "Jean, you've got the number?"

"Somewhere."

Cort left the room, and Jean heard him giving orders. After a moment he ducked his head back into Denise's bedroom.

"What was the name of that boat we saw this morning, Jean?" he asked.

"The *Sugar Daddy*," she told him. "Denise, will you be all right? Will you call if—"

"If the car starts, I'll be all right," Denise proclaimed with her usual bravado, slinging the bag up to her shoulder.

I'm glad you're okay, Jean thought, *because I'm scared out of my skin.*

She gave Denise a brief hug and watched her

leave the apartment with the uniformed police officer. There was nothing to do but to pack her own bag.

"Van Roys dress for dinner," Cort informed her, watching Jean from the doorway of her room as she folded two pairs of jeans.

"I didn't think they were nudists!" Jean grumbled, and suddenly Cort laughed.

"I meant—"

"I know what you meant," Jean snapped. "In fact, I actually have something in my closet Kiki might not look down her nose at."

She crossed the room and took out her favorite pink silk blouse and the gray suit she usually wore with it. Then she moved hangers around until she came to a dress, suitably discreet in dark beige and classically cut. She held her selections up for Cort's approval.

His response was only partially gratifying because halfway through the nod he gave her he turned away. She heard him stalk across the bare floor of the living room to Denise's bedroom.

Jean shrugged, by now almost used to the inexplicable abruptness of Cort's actions. Confident that she probably would be better off not knowing what he was doing, she lay the clothing across the end of her bed and proceeded to find some underwear to take with her.

Her lingerie drawer was nearly empty since Sunday was laundry day, but there on a satiny surface was the imprint of a hand, much larger than her own.

She was about to scream when she thought better of it. Cort would just come to see what the problem was, and she would be embarrassed to have him looking at her lavender teddy, fuchsia nightshirt, and panties of a variety of hues.

Somewhere between her throat and her stomach, she felt the panic that Denise had felt. As Denise had done, she took control of herself and did what she had to do. Quickly she picked out what she needed and packed her suitcase.

Cort was staring at the midnight-blue evening gown hanging on the door of Denise's closet when she found him. He took the hanger off the back of the door, turned the gown around, and searched inside for the tag, which, of course, had been removed by the consignment shop.

"What are you doing!" Jean demanded.

"I just wanted to know . . ."

"Dammit, I don't need any more of this! People going through everything in our apartment! Do you know how it makes Denise and me feel? Denise isn't involved in this. She doesn't deserve your . . . touching her gown."

"I'm sorry," Cort apologized meekly, removing his hand from the fabric.

"We feel . . . violated," Jean complained. "That creep made us feel—What are you going to do about it?"

"I'll catch him," Cort assured her calmly.

"I want in on it!"

"No," Cort argued, hanging the dress once more on the back of the door. "DePesca and Simon are dangerous men. It's no place for an amateur."

"I'm going to help you," Jean stated, even more infuriated because Cort stood staring at the gown.

"It was Denise's gown," Cort mused, not looking at her but running his hand through his black hair.

"Yes."

"Simon assumed it was yours, so he went through Denise's things, thinking he'd find the Rose."

Jean nodded. "Now he knows the Rose is not here, and DePesca had already been taken from the hotel when I had the Rose put in the hotel safe." He turned slowly to face Jean, his dark brows drawn together in a frown. "They think we still have the Rose with us."

"Don't you think they are smart enough to know that you would put it in a safe place?" Jean asked.

Cort looked back at her. "Of course, but logically they would think that would be the safe at Pieter's and we both know it's a sieve!"

"Would they try to enter Pieter's house in daylight?" Jean asked, frightened.

"Let's hope not." Cort reached out to take the

garment bag Jean was carrying. "Jean, would you like to go to the hotel for dinner tonight?"

She saw a spark in his eyes and knew he was working on a plan. "Whatever you say."

"Do you have a large purse that goes with your suit?"

"Of course," Jean replied.

"Bring it," Cort ordered and hurried past her to the living room.

"How long has it been since you slept?" Jean asked Cort when they returned to the house. He had yawned several times in the car and she was worried about him.

"I got up at six yesterday morning because I had a call from Paris. I don't think I've been to bed since."

"Maybe this would be a good time to get a few hours of rest," she suggested.

"I sleep very little when I'm in the middle of a case," Cort told her. He led her into a room where Pieter was watching the Knicks' and the Celtics' basketball game on television. "Besides, I have too much thinking to do, plans to make. Ah, Pieter! Jean is going to have to stay here because her apartment isn't safe."

"Fine," Pieter shrugged.

Kiki looked up from the magazine she was reading on the window seat and glared at them.

"I'm sorry for the inconvenience," Cort apologized.

"I suppose this is part of your messy little investigation," Kiki said with disdain. "It seems the only times you come here you bring trouble with you."

"I'm sorry, but it can't be avoided," Cort explained.

"The room beside yours will have to do," Kiki offered without enthusiasm.

"It will do nicely." Cort turned away.

"We'd planned to eat out tonight," Kiki told them, as though she were enjoying placing another obstacle before them.

"Not to worry," Cort responded lightly. "So had we."

Carrying Jean's garment bag over his shoulder, Cort seemed eager to lead Jean up the winding stairway, past mullioned windows and marble columns.

"I enjoy staying here," Cort confided when they had reached the second floor. "There is so much space, and we can look out at the ocean. Please don't be angry with Kiki for telling you to use this room beside mine. I would have suggested it myself, for your safety. But it looks a bit as if it has just caught all the cast-off furniture from the years this house has been used."

The door of the room was ajar and he pushed it open with his toe. The walls were a mellowed cream and the woodwork painted white, as though at one time the room had been a nursery. With a narrow bed, there was room for a Windsor rocker and a small writing desk.

"Oh, I think it's charming just the way it is," Jean told him, lowering her duffel to the seat of the rocker.

Cort gave her a look that said he thought she was being generous, then turned to hang her garment bag in the closet.

"The bath hasn't been updated much since the house was built," he went on, pointing through the door to a room that featured a claw-foot bathtub and a pedestal sink. "I can deal with it because it's very much like what I am used to in Europe, but here it seems . . . old. We'll have to share. You see, this was the children's suite originally. I'll try not to get in your way."

"Really, Cort," Jean said, reaching out and laying her hand on his arm, "I think it's charming. You've seen where I have been living; this is much nicer than an apartment over a deli."

"I thought the aroma of the deli was divine," he teased, his grin enigmatic.

Jean chuckled and paused to look at the discoloration around his eye, placing her hand on his shoulder.

"Your eye looks a little better, but if you don't get some rest —"

"I don't need rest right now," Cort told her, putting his hands gently on her shoulders. He traced the raised knit pattern of her Irish knit sweater to the collar of her blue striped shirt. "I need . . ."

He kissed her forehead, then surrounded her with his arms and held her to his chest.

"Such a silly thing to bring two people together," he mused. "But until DePesca is out of town, you are in danger, and I want you close to me so I can protect you. But who is going to protect me from you?"

"Protect you from me?" Jean asked, then laughed. "Shouldn't that be the other way around?"

He put her away from him and tilted his head. "I cannot let myself be sidetracked much longer. I have to call my superior in Paris, then I have to make some plans. If you're going to leave your room, let me know."

"I'm going to unpack, then I'll help you make your plans," Jean told him. "I'm serious. I want to be in on everything."

She watched as he checked the locks of the high, mullioned windows that overlooked the ocean, then left by the hallway.

"Don't leave the house under any circumstances," Cort ordered, stern authority in his voice. "Not even to go sit on the patio."

"All right, I won't," Jean agreed. When she heard him enter his room, she sighed. He seemed to be shying away from her, and she wondered why.

Unfortunately she felt as though her thought

processes were being muddled by the lack of sleep and the lazy rhythm of the breakers as they rolled against the seawall beyond the windows.

If she didn't get her unpacking done now, the bed would reach out and grab her.

When she had finished, she stood at the window and watched the span of the ocean. This place seemed so far away from her neighborhood, where daily existence was a challenge. Yet here, here where it seemed so peaceful, there was every bit the danger, perhaps more, if Cort could be believed.

The report of an apartment being broken into would not have gotten such a quick response from the police had not Cort's investigation been involved. It was a sobering thought.

Frankly, she wouldn't want to live like this, with every window wired to a security system, floodlights beaming on the entrances of the houses from dusk to dawn, the threat of robbery and burglary everywhere.

She had often prided herself on not owning anything someone else wanted more than she did. But that vestige of security had been ripped away from her, and now she didn't know where she stood.

Now she had something someone else wanted and was willing to take forcibly, and she needed protection.

She sat down in the Windsor rocker and

rocked it back and forth a few times. Wealth, she thought, had its price.

Cort leaned his shoulders against the headboard of his bed and propped the telephone on his ribs, careful to keep its weight away from a painfully-bruised area. He crossed his ankles and tried to relax while the phone rang on the other end. Finally it was answered.

"Robert, I have a problem," Cort informed him in French, not waiting for his superior to lecture him on what time it was in Paris. This was business, important business, and it had to be dealt with immediately. "I've been compromised."

"How so?" Robert asked, suddenly sounding more alert.

"I've met someone in my investigation whom I cannot ignore, or understand," Cort told him, still not satisfied with the words he was saying. "It's a woman."

Robert chuckled. "As though I had not already guessed."

"She showed up at that party last night wearing one of my family's jewels that has been missing for more than sixty years," he explained. "She's a nobody, as far as society is concerned. She claimed to know nothing about the jewel . . . about jewel thieves . . . about any of this. But DePesca's man, Simon, has already ransacked her apartment, and I can't let her out of my sight, for her own protection."

"And she is probably beautiful, young—" Robert guessed "—ah, to be in the field again . . ."

"I'm serious, Robert," Cort growled. It was too important an issue to joke about. Unless he cut to the bone of his feelings, Robert would not understand the gravity of the situation. "I'm in a compromised position. There's some suspicion attached to this woman, yet I am too attracted to her to think clearly. I certainly do not have my full concentration on the matter of getting DePesca and his cohort out of Palm Beach."

"We can check the woman out easily enough," Robert suggested.

"Even so, I want to resign."

"You're being hasty."

Cort shook his head. "No I'm not. From now on I will always be second-guessing myself when I put myself in danger. I can't be effective in that state of mind."

"Don't be so melodramatic. You'll get over her."

"Robert—"

"I can't allow you to resign at this time. Our department is spread too thin. It's not a good time."

"You have three letters of resignation from me that you have never acted upon," Cort complained in exasperation. "Now I'm asking you again to let me resign."

"And I'm again refusing. Now tell me about this woman, and I'll have all the information about her gathered and sent to you as soon as possible."

Cort frowned and lowered his voice as he told Robert everything he knew about Jeanellen Barbour.

Chapter Five

Jean rapped softly on Cort's door, having waited impatiently for him to stop talking on the telephone. She heard the bedsprings ease and feet hit the floor with a thud. She felt an instant's regret that she had disturbed him because some rest was better than none at all. When he opened the door, he looked at her like a boy who had been caught with his hand in the cookie jar.

"I want to know what the plan is," Jean demanded, not making any move to enter his room.

"Don't worry, it's all under control," he told her and would have turned away.

"Well, tell me what we're doing so I won't make a mistake and wreck everything." She could see by his closed expression that he was not about to share anything with her. "Consider, if you will," she argued, crossing her arms in front of her and leaning against the

99

doorjamb, "the mess I made of your plan last night. Wouldn't you rather I know what is expected of me?"

He nodded slowly, as though thinking something through. "Perhaps you have a point."

He led her to the sitting room at the head of the main stairway and motioned for her to sit down.

"I've decided that it would be best to put the rest of your valuables in the hotel's safe with the Champagne Rose," he advised, sitting down in a chair beside hers. He kept his voice low, as though they were surrounded by spies. "We have no reason to think DePesca knows that the Rose is there, but we cannot guarantee that he won't come searching here tonight."

Jean nodded. "What about Kiki's jewelry?"

"Kiki rarely brings anything of value with her to Palm Beach," Cort said. "She already took anything she is worried about to the bank earlier last week. Remember, she was one of the first to know about DePesca when I, ah, bumped into him last week."

"I see. Do you think he will come tonight?"

Cort leaned back in his chair and stifled a yawn. "Even thieves and scoundrels need to rest sometime," he told her with a chuckle. "Knowing DePesca's thoroughness, he needs a day to find out the best way to get into this house and the most likely location for the safe. He's not a man to blunder through a house aim-lessly."

"Aha!" Jean exclaimed softly. "So this is what is considered taking advantage of an ad-versary's strength?"

His sudden smile warmed her heart, ac-knowledging her grasp of the situation. "You might call it that," Cort agreed. "So, you want to know what I plan to do? You want to help? Then this is what we are going to do."

Twilight had cast its long shadows over the Atlantic Ocean. Jean reluctantly pulled herself away from the view to bathe and dress for din-ner.

She hadn't heard much from the direction of Cort's room, so she assumed he had taken her advice to get some sleep. She was pleased that he was being reasonable. She detected a rash, untamed streak in him, a tendency to disregard any advice he didn't agree with. Not that that was unattractive. She liked a man who thought for himself, who was not easily swayed by whim and hormones. In her experience they were few and far between.

Cort was unique in her experience. She ac-cepted this interlude in her life with gratitude for whatever short time their lives were inter-twined. She knew in her mind that it would not last. But her heart did not agree.

She had time to French-braid her long blond hair, although it involved unbraiding several times before she was pleased with what she saw in the triple mirror over the small dresser. When she finally heard the shower running in the bathroom, Jean dug a bottle of polish from her purse and did her nails.

By the time Cort knocked gently on her door, she was so rested that she was beginning to get nervous.

"Are you ready?"

Jean opened the door while she blew on her right hand one last time. Her next breath caught in her throat as she looked up at Cort's face. In the dim light of the hallway he looked incredibly handsome, his tanned face rested and self-assured.

"What do you think?" Jean asked him seriously, turning once so he could see the full effect of her neat-but-elegant costume. She certainly didn't want to embarrass him.

"Ohh! How do you do that with your hair?" Cort asked, admiration in his voice.

Jean pressed her palm to her mouth to stifle a giggle. "Very carefully!"

Cort took her hand in his and kissed it. "I should have known you would look perfect," he complimented. "Get your purse."

She followed him to the library, where he had stashed her jewelry in the wall safe. Opening the safe from the combination he had memorized that morning, he carefully removed the pieces of jewelry and placed them on a linen handkerchief.

Jean interfered to retrieve the silver cabbage rose, over his unvoiced objections.

"You can't have this one," she told him firmly, with a slight tone of triumph. "This outfit is made for it."

"It is, yes," Cort murmured.

She draped the soft collar of her silky pink blouse aside and secured it to the lapel of her jacket with the pin.

"You are a very stylish woman, Jean. I like that. Perhaps it's best that you wear something stunning like this rose. It will further our deception."

He folded the handkerchief closed and handed it to her. "Put this in your purse and guard it with . . ."

The words "your life" hung in the air between them, unsaid. His gray eyes grew deathly serious.

"You don't think it will come to that, do you?" Jean asked lightly.

"I hope not," Cort replied, turning away to close the safe. He took out another handkerchief and wiped his fingerprints from the handle.

"Why are you doing that?" Jean asked.

"So there will be only one set of fingerprints on it if someone else opens it," he told her.

"Of course, almost everyone uses gloves, but there's always a chance that a criminal will make a fatal mistake."

She nodded and let him take her arm. There were moments when all this intrigue made her knees weak. Perhaps if she just put one foot ahead of the other and held her head up she could carry off his plan with some of the style he seemed to admire.

Although she was even more awed by the opulence that surrounded her, Jean tried to look unimpressed when the maître d' led them to a linen-draped table under a crystal chandelier in the hotel's main dining room. From the pleased look on Cort's face as he glanced around the room and took his place across the table from her, she could see that his plan was setting up to his satisfaction.

Jean was a little disconcerted when the waiter removed the white linen napkin from the water goblet at her place, unfurled it with a flourish, and draped it across her lap. He filled the glass from a heavy crystal pitcher, then without missing a beat performed the same service for Cort, who seemed unaffected by the whole ritual.

"I find the lobster here exceptional, but so is the prime rib," Cort recommended, studying the menu.

"I've always wondered what coq au vin would be like," Jean mused.

"Oh? Well, that settles that, then," Cort decided. "You should take advantage of having your curiosity satisfied."

Through the soup course, Jean didn't have the feeling Cort was on his guard as much as he had been the night before. His attention to her was thorough but not overwhelming.

Jean had never thought she could be comfortable with someone she was attracted to, but the past twenty-four hours had been full of surprises. One more barely made a difference.

The manager of the hotel stopped by the table and nonchalantly engaged Cort in what seemed to be an inconsequential conversation. Cort nodded meaningfully toward Jean.

With carefully-controlled movements she took the jewelry from her purse and passed the still-folded cloth to Cort, being careful to keep the exchange below the level of the tabletop.

Almost at the same time the manager took his own handkerchief from his inside pocket and patted it to his forehead. With an economy of movement that would have done credit to a magician, he returned the handkerchief to his inside pocket, where it now surrounded the cache of jewelry on its way to the hotel safe.

Cort seemed very relieved when the whole transaction was finished. He ordered chocolate mousse for dessert.

Jean caught her breath and picked up her purse from her lap.

"I think I'll powder my nose," Jean excused herself, needing a moment alone to still the thumping of her heart.

"Can it wait the slightest moment?" Cort asked.

Jean questioned him with her eyes as he glanced casually around the room.

At last he nodded. "Be very careful," Cort cautioned, lowering his voice and leaning across the table in an intimate pose. "You're still wearing two pieces of valuable antique jewelry, Jean. I should not have let you keep that ring and the silver rose, but you seem to love them so much that I don't have the heart to take them from you."

To a casual observer, they looked like lovers exchanging some private words in the candlelight.

Cort patted her hand. "Be very careful," he repeated.

His admonition did nothing to still the churning of Jean's emotions as she sought the sanctuary of the elaborate powder room. Her nerves were further frayed when she sensed someone hurrying behind her to the same destination.

When she reached a mirrored wall, she saw the reflection of the woman she had seen here the evening before, taking thorough notes

106

about the people at the party.

It was only her instinct for self-preservation that made her turn and confront the woman. "May I ask exactly what you're doing?" Jean demanded.

The woman looked at her with raised eyebrows, then straightened her shoulders. "I'm an information gatherer for a writer of a nationally-syndicated society column," she told Jean in a challenging tone. "I'm covering the season here for her."

"Hm." Jean took a deep breath and felt some tension drift out of her. She chose to believe the woman. "Tell me," she asked, motioning toward two chairs in an alcove, "did you see an incident last night? A man removed from the premises by security people? The police?"

The woman moistened her lips and perched tentatively on one of the little chairs. "Yes. He was graceful enough to leave without too much of a scene."

"What did he look like?" Jean asked, folding her hands together in her lap to keep them from trembling.

"Fortyish," the woman told her reflectively. "Probably European, slightly balding, dark hair, pasty complexion, and close beard. It was the eyes that told me he is a criminal. Oh, he was suitably dressed, but he was definitely out of place in that crowd. I saw scabs on the knuckles of his right hand. Do you know who he is?"

Jean bit her lower lip. "I don't know him, no."

"Do you know his name?"

"I know what he is called," Jean responded. "But I'm not at liberty to tell you."

"The gentleman you are with? Pieter van Roy's cousin? Cort van Roy, isn't he—"

"Yes," Jean answered quickly, knowing that she was now caught in the trap of quid pro quo. She had received information from this woman and had to reciprocate.

She dreaded giving away some information that would jeopardize Cort's mission. More than that, she could not bear it if this woman told her that Cort was just another opportunist traveling with the moneyed set.

"Has he let anything slip about the rumors of Pieter and Kiki breaking up?" the columnist asked.

Jean felt a twinge. Here was a chance to do good or evil, and she must say something.

Jean straightened the ring on her right hand, seemingly studying it to give herself time to think. Then she looked at the woman again and smiled.

"Really, I can't imagine how those rumors got started," Jean said with a light laugh. "Pieter and Kiki seem as close as they were when I first met them."

"But everyone's been saying—"

"Now I really have to get back to Cort," Jean stated, hastily getting to her feet.

The journalist laughed knowingly. "Personally, I wouldn't leave him alone for very long myself. Thank you. I hope we run into each other again before the season is over."

I won't hold my breath, Jean thought as she hurried from the rest room.

As they lingered over coffee, Jean and Cort listened to the guitarist in the corner strum Bach etudes while tables were cleared.

"It's nice to just come to a full stop and enjoy the evening, isn't it?" Cort mused, reaching across the table and taking Jean's hand.

"Yes," she agreed, wondering if he expected some sort of response that she did not know. His eyes were intense and directed only at her. She glanced away momentarily to avoid their heat and to gain control of her wild imagination.

Across the room, the woman whom she had encountered in the ladies' room looked back at her with interest.

Jean moistened her lips discreetly and smiled back at Cort. "This is a lovely place to spend an evening," she said to fill the silence between the quiet guitar pieces.

"You make it lovely," Cort told her, raising

her hand to his lips.

Jean took a deep breath. She was mesmerized by the directness of his gaze, her heart captured just as he had captured her hand. She felt as though she would explode from the intensity of his attention.

Then at a signal from the manager standing in the doorway, he looked around for the waiter and asked for the check.

So much for outrageous flirtation, Jean thought, reaching for her purse. *It's back to earth and reality.*

The waiter brought the little folder with the bill in it on a silver tray. Cort removed a piece of paper that was under the bill—the receipt for the jewelry just placed in the hotel safe—and put it into his wallet when he had selected the credit card he wanted to use. It was a bit of legerdemain that would have made a cardsharp proud.

Had she not taken Cort's arm, Jean never would have been able to put one foot ahead of the other to leave the hotel. The breeze that swept through the street did little to cool the fire that was glowing inside her. If she was to survive this encounter with Cort and the life he represented, she needed to restore calm, clear thinking to the situation. She needed distance.

But Cort did not let Jean more than a few inches away from him the whole way back to the mansion. He drove slowly through the streets, taking the time to admire the lighted lawns they passed.

"You see the main method of security in this neighborhood," he pointed out. "Floodlights." He shrugged. "I guess it works well enough."

The van Roy mansion was brilliantly lighted, also, and Cort looked at the arrangement of lights critically.

"I just hope DePesca and Simon are as tired as I am," he said, letting them into the house. "I do need some sleep."

"So do I," Jean told him. "Do you think your friends will take the night off?"

"I hope so. I imagine right now they are trying to decide if there is anything in town worth scheming for. Frankly, everything should be pretty much locked up by now. At least, all your important jewelry is safe."

"Are you sure Kiki's is safe?" Jean asked, knowing the matter was already settled but trying to prolong their conversation while Cort loosened his tie.

Cort laughed. "She learned in her early days not to carry anything she can't afford to lose."

"Well, I guess I haven't learned that one yet," Jean muttered, begrudging Kiki points on anything.

"There's time," Cort assured her, suddenly hugging her with one arm and kissing her temple.

"Oh, I thought I heard you," Pieter greeted

111

them, coming to the doorway. "Come on into the family room. We're watching family video-tapes and eating popcorn."

"What do you think?" Cort whispered, turning to Jean. "Mind being bored for a little while?"

"I'm game if you are," Jean chuckled. "But keep me away from the popcorn."

"We'll be there in a minute," Cort told Pieter.

When Pieter had left, Cort turned back to Jean, resting his arm casually around her waist. "We don't have to join them, you know. We could . . . find another place to sit and talk."

"Of course we could," Jean agreed. "But that would be rude, on my part at least. Really, I don't mind."

"We do need to sit down and have a serious discussion this evening, though," Cort told her. "There are decisions to be made."

Jean frowned. "Yes, I guess so."

"Jean, I know that you are probably not comfortable being so dressed up, and I could do without this jacket. Why don't you go upstairs and change your clothes and drop this jacket off in my room and bring me the sweater that's lying on the foot of the bed," he suggested, handing over his blazer.

Jean winced again at seeing the holster strapped to his side. "Must you wear that gun?" she asked, and immediately felt contrite.

"Yes," he informed her softly. "It's for your own protection as well as mine and the rest of the household's. Don't be afraid of it. The safety is on and it is not a hair-trigger. Tomorrow I'll teach you how to use it, and then you won't mind so much."

Jean glowered back at him.

"It will take more than learning to use it."

"I'm glad you care that much," Cort said, with his maddeningly endearing lopsided grin. He tilted his head toward the stairway. "Hurry back."

Cort sank into one of the couches in the family room and glanced at the oversized television screen. On the screen a towheaded boy played a rather complicated piano piece to the ticking of a metronome. He was dwarfed by the instrument he played.

"Willie is getting very good, isn't he?" Pieter noted proudly when his son finished the piece.

"How old is he now?" Cort asked.

"He'll be eight in March, just after we get back from Cannes," Kiki told him with a wistful smile.

"You wouldn't want to miss his birthday," Cort said, hoping that he could sidetrack Pieter from any judgment of the boy's playing.

"No, we never do," Kiki bragged. "The housekeeper makes a tape every week so we can keep up on his progress with the piano, and see him playing in the snow. We can't take him out of school, though, not for three whole months."

Cort frowned. He'd been brought up the same way, in private academies, his parents gone for long periods of time with the diplomatic service. Maybe traveling was in the van Roy genes, like blond hair that sometimes turned very black around age fifteen, or stayed wispily sparse.

"So, do you send him tapes of what you are doing here?" Cort wondered.

Kiki and Pieter looked at each other. "No," Pieter replied. "We never thought of it."

"Besides," Kiki went on with a shrug, "what could we show him?"

"This!" Cort said, another plan forming. "A cozy evening, watching tapes of him, eating popcorn by the fire. He'll love it! Where's your video cam?"

"Why didn't we ever think of it?" Pieter asked with a laugh, going to a cabinet and rummaging through it.

Cort followed him to the cabinet and picked up a still camera that was nearby. "You have this, too, huh? Is there any film in it?"

"There should be," Pieter responded, checking the battery pack of the video camera.

"I'll take some photos of you two, then," Cort offered. He took the cover off the lens

114

and checked the film indicator to be sure it was loaded.

He glanced over his shoulder when Jean entered the room. She was wearing the same blouse she had worn to dinner over a pair of gray slacks. He raised the camera to his right eye and framed her in the viewfinder.

This had been easier than he had expected. He'd have a picture of Miss Jeanellen Barbour to fax to Robert before noon tomorrow.

"Hey! I thought you were going to take a picture of us?" Pieter said, nudging Cort's ribs.

Cort's wince of pain was hidden behind the camera. He'd almost forgotten about those ribs.

"I found a nice subject," Cort observed with a glint in his eyes. "Come on, Kiki, move a little closer to the television and I'll get a picture of you watching Willie on the tape."

"We'll have to get you on the tape, too, Cort," Pieter said as he started the video camera. "Willie is one of your biggest fans. He says he wants to be a spy."

"I am not a spy!" Cort corrected. "Please get that idea out of his head. I am an investigator with one of the most prestigious and honorable agencies in the world."

"Oh, my, we touched a nerve!" Kiki drawled.

He snapped her picture. As soon as the camera had wound the film, he turned and took a picture of Jean, catching her off guard and almost full-face.

Damn his training. Damn having to hold suspicions about someone he cared as much about as Jean. Damn the subterfuges and the secrecy and the uncertainty of drawing his next breath. Damn all the years he hadn't known her and all the nights of the rest of his life when she would be somewhere else.

"Thank you for bringing me the sweater, Jean," Cort said, putting the camera down. "We mustn't give Willie the idea that my pistol is part of my everyday costume."

After they had made a short tape, they sat around and watched it. It was pretty tame stuff, and not well done, but — Pieter kept saying — it was for Willie's benefit, and he wouldn't be so critical.

Kiki sat in her highbacked chair, her legs drawn up under her, a frown creasing her forehead.

"Is something wrong?" Cort asked her gently as Pieter put all the equipment away.

"Yes," Kiki answered. "But for once I know what to do about it. Look, if you can all look after yourselves, I'm going to bed."

"Sure," Pieter said, closing the cabinet. "I'll be up in a minute. Cort, there is one more exposure on that roll in the still camera. Let me take a picture of you and Jean, right there on the couch. Move in a little closer. . . . Ah! That's it."

116

"I'll take the film to be developed tomorrow," Cort offered.

"Would you? That would be great. I, ah, don't think you two need me around, do you? You know where the bar is, where the kitchen is . . ." Pieter unloaded the camera and put the film into a little canister.

Cort reached out to him, and Pieter dropped the film into his hand. Cort slipped it into the pocket of his slacks.

Pieter didn't waste much time leaving the room. There was an awkward moment when Cort wondered if Jean would decide she'd had a long enough day, also.

But she sat staring into the fire, much as she had during the odd moments in the past hour when the conversation had not engaged her.

"We have to talk," Cort reminded her. "And I think I need something to drink. Do you?"

"Nothing, thank you," Jean said. "I need a clear head. But don't deprive yourself on my account."

Cort chuckled and got them each a glass of wine.

"You don't have to drink that," he said, putting the glass on the table in front of Jean. "It's a fair year, but it was the last full glass in the bottle and I couldn't see it going to waste."

"Thank you," Jean murmured.

"I am coming to terms with the fact that the van Roy Roses are out of the family's hands

117

and that you are the legal owner of them. I wish it were otherwise, but I do not hold any bad feelings toward you about that."

"Good," Jean said, but her tone told him that something was bothering her. "I've been having to face a few realizations about the Roses myself. For a long time the figures you gave me, appraising the diamond rose in particular, didn't sink in. Then I realized what a big responsibility is involved in keeping something as valuable as that."

He nodded in agreement.

"I hope I am an intelligent person," she told him. "And prudent. I don't think I make enough money in a year to properly insure the diamond, let alone the rest of the jewelry. It means something to me, though, and parting with it will be a wrench. I will always have the memories of playing with it in my grandmother's sewing room while she made clothes for me. But I know that I have to let it go."

Cort felt his heart thump, as much in surprise as in sympathy with the sadness he heard in her voice. He reached for her hand and gently folded it into his own.

"That might be wisest," he told her. "While you own it, it will only be a worry to you.

"That's what I was thinking." Jean's free hand went to the silver rose on the collar of her pink blouse. "I'll never let go of this silver rose, though. It's not as ostentatious or valuable as the diamond, but it means even more to me. Through the years that I've had it, I've always had one outfit that I planned around it. I've given it a lot of thought, Cort, and I can't let it go."

"I understand."

"But what is the best way to get rid of the diamond?" Jean asked.

"Certainly not to sell it locally," Cort advised, thinking quickly.

A plan had instantly popped into his mind, but he did not want to tell her all of it. He hated to deceive her, yet it was necessary.

"You would never get what it is worth here," he explained. "There is an auction house in Antwerp where it would get the attention it deserves and you would get the fairest price. It would take a little time, of course."

"That's all right," Jean responded. "I'm not in a great hurry, I have my job, so I'm not destitute."

Cort chuckled. "I love your attitude."

"I have an attitude?"

"Some people would be jumping out of their skins to capitalize on such a find," he pointed out.

"I'm not exactly calm about it."

"Tell me," he said, letting go of her hand to put his arm around her shoulder and draw her closer. "What are you planning to do with all that money?"

"Certainly not count it before it's in my hand," Jean stated. "But I might open a little boutique or gift shop."

"Here? On Worth Avenue?"

Jean laughed. "No! Maybe back home or . . . somewhere."

"Paris? New York?"

"No, I'm a small-town person. I've decided I don't like it much here. It might be time to move on."

"Are you sure you're not a van Roy?" he asked teasingly. "We all have wanderlust."

"Maybe I am." Jean laughed.

Cort looked down into her eyes for a long moment. That might be how the Roses got out of the family. They were not really out of the family but merely held in a branch that was not—

He put the thought away from him as unworthy. He didn't want to think about it now.

He had wanted to touch the strands of her blond hair that strayed from the elaborate braid at the back of her head. He wanted to kiss her lips and to feel the silk of her blouse against his cheek.

"Your eye," Jean whispered, touching this bruise with her fingertips. "Does it still hurt?"

"Sometimes."

"Do Dutch mamas kiss little boo-boos to

120

make them well?"

"It's universal!" he chuckled.

She kissed his bruise and looked back at him with a challenge in her smile.

"I have a lump here, too." Cort tapped his finger at the corner of his mouth.

"Ah . . ." Jean sympathized, then kissed him, a kiss he joined in eagerly.

The only way he wanted her to be a van Roy was by marriage!

Chapter Six

Cort leaned closer to Jean and kissed her as though theirs was a long-standing affection. Jean touched his cheek when he backed away slightly and smiled into his gray eyes.

"I thought you wanted to talk," she said.

"We talked," he murmured as though everything between them was settled.

Jean frowned at him and laughed softly in disbelief. "I didn't think we accomplished much with our discussion."

"I'd rather kiss you." He shrugged. "Can I help it if you are beautiful in this light and I want to kiss you, embrace you? That is the word, isn't it? It's almost the same in French."

Jean chuckled and shook her head slowly. "There are some things that don't have to be translated, I guess."

Cort pulled her into his arms and kissed her lips gently, as though this was the first time they had kissed. Jean smiled to herself. Her fears of being in over her head were unfounded.

She twined her arms around his neck, and he rested his cheek on the silk of her sleeve for an instant. She realized she truly knew nothing about him and that her heart was making decisions for her that her head should overrule.

She set her boundaries for their intimacy, and he respected them. When his hand strayed from her waist to the underswell of her breast, she brushed his hand away. He looked at her for a long moment, then nodded, perhaps sadly.

But the issue was settled, and as she walked slowly to her room later, she had no regrets.

Jean was roused by an unfamiliar alarm clock in the unfamiliar bedroom. It took her a few seconds to remember everything that had happened in the last two days.

It was just another Monday morning. She had to work at Ben Evans's print shop, no matter how much she would like to loll around and pretend she was a van Roy.

Jean showered, rebraided her hair in an easy style, and donned jeans, tossing a colorful blouse over her T-shirt in hopes of making it more presentable until she got to work.

The house was very quiet as she sauntered across the thick carpeting of the upstairs hallway and down the curving stairway to the first floor. About the only sounds she heard were shuffling footsteps and quiet humming beyond the kitchen door.

She found Mrs. Ghent in the spacious kitchen, carefully measuring ground coffee into a coffeemaker.

The cook turned and glared at her as Jean entered, then she smiled and nodded toward the machine. "This'll be ready in about five minutes, if you can wait that long."

"Of course," Jean said. "What can I help you with?"

"Miss, a guest doesn't generally come into this kitchen and offer help," Mrs. Ghent scolded mildly.

"I have to get to work. I'm not used to this kind of life," Jean confided. "I don't know how to act. My great-grandmother was a day lady, and my grandmother did housework for people, too, when she was really young. But I just never paid much attention to how things were done in high society like this."

"It's the ones who haven't got the sense to care about people that make a job like this difficult," Mrs. Ghent told her. "You ain't been no trouble at all to me and the maid, so that's in your favor. I don't cotton to people messing up my kitchen, though. I'd rather serve seven courses to twelve people than to have someone pour himself a cup of coffee in my kitchen."

"Sorry," Jean apologized, backing toward the garden room. "I'll get out of your way and—"

The door opened as she was about to reach for it and Cort looked inside. "So there you are!"

"Good morning," she managed to say, studying his left eye to see if the swelling and discoloration had been reduced by a night of rest. "Your eye looks a little better."

"What are you doing in here?"

"Getting kicked out of Mrs. Ghent's way," Jean retorted with a grin, going out into the garden room. "Where can I find a phone book so I can call a cab to take me to work?"

He caught her arm in his hand and stopped her from going toward the library. "You're not going to work today," he said authoritatively.

"Cort, I have to make a living," she told him. "I get paid by the hour, eight-thirty to five every day, sometimes even Saturday. No work, no pay, do you understand?"

"Yes, but there are things to do today that only you can do," Cort said. "I had a wild idea that we might go for a real sail—after we take your jewelry to a bank and place it in a safety-deposit box."

"It sounds like fun," Jean mused wistfully. "The sail, I mean, not carrying the jewelry all over town. But Ben's busy in the print shop this time of year."

"Can you call him and tell him that you'll be in around ten?" Cort asked. "Banks don't open until nine."

"I need my job, Cort. Ben isn't very understanding when it comes to unexpected time off, especially for frivolous reasons."

"And making sure that your jewelry is secure is a frivolous reason?" Cort demanded, a flash of the anger she had seen in him Saturday night surfacing in his eyes.

"I might point out that all those pieces have has been perfectly fine in a candy box for several years—"

"Until you had the audacity to crash a party you shouldn't have gone to."

"I shouldn't have gone to?" she demanded, bristling. "Because I'm not good enough to mingle with rich people?"

"I didn't mean that!"

"Coffee?" Mrs. Ghent asked cheerfully, bringing a tray from the kitchen. She seemed pleased to have interrupted their argument. "Would either of you like eggs this morning?"

"Yes," Cort replied.

"No," Jean countered, unable to even contemplate breakfast at the moment. "I don't have time."

"Jean, please call your boss and ask for a little time," Cort pleaded. "I'll have you back at the shop by eleven at the latest."

"Oh, all right." Jean reached for the phone.

"Hot cereal, Miss Jean?" Mrs. Ghent asked.

"No, just toast or something."

"Maybe some fruit," Mrs. Ghent proposed.

126

"Yes, fine," Jean capitulated, mostly to settle the matter before Ben answered his phone and took her head off for wanting a couple of hours to go to the bank.

When she had hung up after the disagreeable conversation, she sat down at the place Mrs. Ghent had set for her and poured a little cream into her coffee.

"I'm sorry." Cort sighed heavily. "Perhaps I'm too used to people doing what I tell them, always, without question. It's strange to find someone who doesn't think what I feel is important is really necessary. Yes, you could carry your jewelry around in a candy box for years, but the van Roy Rose has been spotted. If De-Pesca doesn't try to steal it, someone else will."

"All right! I said I'd do what you want me to," Jean exploded.

"And I'm trying to apologize."

"I thought you were lecturing."

"I probably was." Cort chuckled. "I'm not good at apologizing; I'm good at lecturing."

Mrs. Ghent returned from the kitchen with a quarter of a cantaloupe garnished with strawberries and grapes. She placed it in front of Jean, along with a danish that looked for all the world as though it had come from Freeman's Deli.

In the congested morning traffic, Cort proved

to be an impatient driver. He fretted that the place where he wanted to drop off his film was a few minutes late opening its doors. He was breathless when he returned to the car. He was almost as edgy waiting for the manager of the hotel to take him to the vault to retrieve the jewelry.

Jean expected him, therefore, to be just as anxious to leave the hotel and get to the bank. Instead, he spread the pieces out on the manager's desk. Cort demanded that she examine each piece to be certain no chicanery had taken place.

"Oh, for heaven's sake!" Jean exclaimed in exasperation as she handed the van Roy Rose back to him. "What is the point of this? Everything is exactly like it was last night and the night before."

"Jean, you are too trusting. Now, put all of this into your purse very carefully."

He straightened his shoulders, and his right hand went into his blazer. In the stillness of the office she heard his signet ring click against his pistol.

"Are you expecting trouble?" Jean asked.

"No," Cort replied, taking her arm, "but I'm ready for it."

He was much more careful as he drove to the bank that he had deemed worthy of guarding her cache. His face was grim and his eyes constantly alert to the cars around him. After helping Jean from the car, he walked into the bank with his left arm around her. It was as though Cort feared she would be in mortal danger if he let her one more inch away from his side.

In definite if subdued tones made all the arrangements for the box, though greatly annoyed at the paperwork involved.

"Do you want both names on the box, or just one?" the teller asked.

"Just Miss Barbour's."

"No," Jean contradicted. "If you don't have your name on it, you won't be able to go into the vault. I'm sure you're going to want to inspect everything."

"How do you know this?" Cort asked.

"I just do."

"Can it be written that I can go into the vault?"

The teller frowned. "Maybe."

"Cort, don't make an issue—"

"But—"

"Put your name down."

When they were let into the safe, Cort studied the interior as though he were about to apply a coat of paint to it.

Jean shivered in the air-conditioning and tried to feel at ease. She was certain that a dowager who had passed them was appalled by her work clothes, probably thinking that Palm Beach certainly wasn't what it once was.

They were shown to a little room, and behind its closed door Cort checked the pieces against an inventory list, in triplicate. They both initialed the lists to show they agreed on the contents. Cort folded one list and placed it in the box, then handed a copy to Jean. He put the third sheet in his own pocket.

Jean didn't dare say she thought he was being overly cautious, because she guessed that he wasn't. He had good, solid reasons for everything he was doing.

They went back to the car, a little farther apart than they had been when they walked into the bank. Jean felt curious relief. She had been telling herself that the jewelry really didn't matter to her. The gems were just objects, not something that was vital to her existence. But now she was glad they were safe.

She glanced at the dashboard clock in the car while Cort was fussing with the seat belt.

"I didn't know it was so late," she lamented.

"So I must finally take you home from the ball," Cort said, and she heard regret in his voice.

She studied him for a long moment as he checked the mirrors. He glanced around the parking lot, perhaps still searching for a familiar car. Did he mean that he wanted to spend more time with her, or did he regret that the chase was over?

"So, what will you do with the rest of your

day?" Jean asked, checking the traffic on her side of the street as they left the lot.

"Go back and pick up the film," he ticked off, "then see if Pieter is going out on his boat. Or maybe I'll play tennis with him on his court."

Jean smiled, imagining how he would look in tennis shorts.

"I envy you," she told him, thinking about the projects that she would be taking on that day. None of them was particularly challenging, just tedious.

Cort insisted on going into the print shop and talking to Ben, taking the heat for the time she had lost that morning.

She could see from the expression on Ben's face that he didn't believe a word Cort said. Indeed, he shouldn't have, because it was nowhere near the truth. That would have sent Ben into a laughing fit or apoplexy—she didn't care to speculate which.

And Cort seemed put off by the grime and the noise of the print shop. Jean saw the place through his eyes at that moment, felt the heat, and almost choked on the dusty air. She didn't wonder that he left quickly, with only a backward glance toward her, promising he would return at quitting time.

"He's quite a character, your new man," Ben observed as Jean perched on the stool at her bench.

131

"He's not my man," Jean informed him, "new or old."

Ben gave her a look that said he thought he knew better. Then he showed Jean what he wanted her to do with a new order.

In the moments that Jean had to think of herself that day, it began to grate on her that Cort did not approve of the place where she worked. She was annoyed that he could not appreciate the kind of life she had to live.

His family—at least his cousin—was rich enough to idle away months of their lives in the sun while others froze in the snowy latitudes. She didn't mind working, and working hard to support herself. Sometimes there was a challenge involved. After all, he earned a living, too.

So why was he looking down his nose at the print shop, just as Kiki had done?

For all his protestations and claims of being a common man, he was as big a snob as his cousin's wife.

Cort opened the envelope of pictures and sifted through them to find the one he had taken of Jean. He held it to the light and studied the likeness, nearly a full-face shot. The soft backlighting of a lamp accentuated the way stray blond hairs had escaped from her elaborate braid.

Her face held little expression at the moment

he had caught her, and it was just as well. He didn't particularly want his superior in Paris seeing the way she looked at him when they were alone. This would be, perhaps, enough ammunition for Robert to make his life miserable for a while. And when he left Jean, he would be miserable enough without anyone else knowing about his pain.

"How long would it take to make an enlargement of this photo?" he asked the clerk.

"I could have it later today," the clerk said, looking over the work he had before him. "No, maybe I'd better not promise it until ten tomorrow morning."

Cort tried to think if he would still be in Palm Beach the next morning, decided that he would be, and nodded.

"I want it . . . this size." He pointed to a sample on the counter, then handed the batch of negatives to the clerk.

"It will come out a little paler than the original," the clerk warned as he wrote up the order. "You have to expect that."

Everything pales in comparison to the subject, he thought with a rueful smile.

If all he was to have of Jean for the rest of his life was this picture, it would have to be enough.

He brooded as he drove to the police station and conferred with Detective Rolland, the liaison officer with whom he had worked on the security for Casino Night.

"And what of the young woman?" Rolland asked, after he had brought Cort up to date on the whereabouts of Stefano DePesca and his henchman, Simon.

"Her jewelry is safe," Cort told him. "Whether she is or not, I don't know. She insisted on going to work as though nothing is happening."

"Maybe, for her, it's for the best to be busy, going about a normal routine," the detective said, running his hand over his balding head. "Laymen can't always bear up under the strain."

"I feel it in my bones that DePesca is just lying low," Cort mused, "perhaps wanting us to think that he's left town, before he makes a strike."

"And where do you think he will strike?"

"I'm hoping it will be where I will be," Cort responded, smiling a bit lopsidedly. His lip still had a small lump in it, although the bruise did not show. It was just a nuisance when he shaved and smiled.

"Now, I must fax this picture of Jeanellen Barbour to my supervisor in Paris," he said, showing the picture to Rolland. "Have you gotten anything about her?"

The man shook his head. "She's as clean as a whistle far as we can tell."

Rolland looked at the picture for a long moment and pressed his lips together in a stern line. "That doesn't mean much, though, considering the short time we've had to work on her file. Sure is pretty, though, isn't she?"

Cort felt his insides tighten at this remark. He wished he was the only one who recognized Jean's beauty. And there was a part of her he felt only he had seen.

He waited at the police station to see if Robert would respond to his faxed message. When he realized how late in the day it was in Paris, Cort conceded that a speedy reply was probably not forthcoming.

Thrusting his hands deep into his pockets, he strolled out to his car, his thoughts so much on Jean that he almost did not resurrect his guarded attitude.

Damn! She'll be the death of me if I don't stop thinking of her. The thought came to him as he unlocked his car and slid inside.

"Leave my car where it is," Cort told his man when he was once more within the gates of the van Roy mansion. "I'll be going out again this afternoon."

José nodded and reached for a squeegee to clean the windshield. "How's the fuel?"

"Fine. Before you do anything else, though," Cort suggested, "go through the house and check all the window locks and door bolts, and the alarm system."

135

"Good, sir, right away." He looked at the sponge in his hand and dropped it back in the bucket. "I can do this later."

Cort walked into the middle of an argument in the family room. Nevertheless, he handed the envelope of pictures he'd had developed to Kiki, who was nearest the door.

Hardly losing a beat, Kiki shuffled through the pictures, keeping up her harangue.

"I didn't mind coming to Florida when we could bring Willie," she stated, her eyes narrowed and hard. "But I was miserable last year when we had to leave him at home, and I'm miserable this year."

"Oh, spare me, Kiki!" Pieter countered. "You're not that dedicated a mother! You just miss—"

"Don't tell me what I miss! I miss Willie! I miss reading stories to him at night and combing his hair in the morning."

"God, that's what we have Hortense for!"

"No, that is not what we have Hortense for! She's a housekeeper and a cook, not a substitute mother. I wouldn't mind leaving Florida and never coming back to this place of social vipers and hedonists."

"You've never been above gossip," Pieter argued. "Nor are you ever adverse to having money spent on you and squandering your time on your own amusements. So where does this unrest come from so suddenly? I think you're being hypocritical."

Kiki snorted and sat down on the couch to contemplate the pictures Cort had handed her.

Cort was never comfortable when he was caught in the crossfire of other people's arguments. He was particularly unsettled when Kiki and Pieter argued. Ten years before, they had been the perfect couple. Cort had stood beside Pieter at his wedding, overcome with his own loneliness when he witnessed their kiss at the end of the ceremony.

He had never thought of them in terms of being dissatisfied with their marriage until he had walked into the house a week ago and felt the tension.

If Kiki and Pieter were having trouble, why should he think of marriage? Why think even of love?

"I . . . I'm sorry I've intruded," Cort apologized.

Pieter and Kiki looked at him as though they had not realized he was in the room. Pieter's face became ruddy and he turned away. Kiki lifted the pictures from her lap.

"Thank you for having the pictures developed," she said, trying to re-establish her dignity. "They're very good. I want to send some of them to Willie."

"I'm having my man check all the window locks," Cort informed them. "He'll check the alarm system, too. You'd better call the security

137

people and tell them what's going on so they won't call the police unnecessarily."

Pieter turned slowly toward him, his eyes searching Cort's. "You're expecting that DePesca character to show up here, aren't you?"

"Yes, and I think we'd better make some changes in the schedule." Cort began to pace. "You usually eat at eight. I think tonight you should eat early so the servants will be out of the house shortly after dark."

Pieter and Kiki looked at each other, fear in their eyes in varying degrees.

"Do you want us to leave, too?" Pieter asked.

"No. I'd rather know where you are."

Kiki shook her head and looked back down at the pictures in her hands. "This is another reason I don't like it here. Jewel thieves don't prey on us in Connecticut. I don't have to worry every time I leave the house. I can go to the hairstylist without hearing all sorts of horror stories about houses being burgled. And people aren't being mugged and beaten up."

Suddenly she looked up at Cort with such pain in her eyes that he almost apologized for being beaten up by Stefano DePesca the week before.

She got to her feet unsteadily and handed the pictures to Pieter. "I'll go tell Mrs. Ghent that we're eating early. She'll probably be upset."

"I'll explain everything to her, if you want me to," Cort offered.

138

Kiki eyed him coldly as she hurried past him. Her heels managed to make a decidedly angry sound even on the carpet.

Pieter sighed and slapped the pictures down on a nearby table.

"I just don't understand her anymore," he complained. "She always loves coming to Florida, loves Cannes in March, Maine in August. But this year all she does is grouse and say she wants to go home."

"Maybe she's not feeling well," Cort supplied lamely.

"Who knows?" Pieter asked. "Who can figure women out?"

Cort chuckled in ironic agreement.

He certainly had not figured Jean out. She was either very simple and straightforward, or the best little con artist he had ever seen. She'd stolen a part of him, and he had not even realized it. She had a style of her own, but she also had boundaries she was cautious about breaching. She was a new experience to him.

Maybe she was right to have boundaries, though. Perhaps marriage wasn't what it was supposed to be. If Kiki and Pieter could be at each other's throats when they had been so much in love before, what chance did he have with Jean?

He was thirty-four and had never been married. He told himself that it was because his job was too dangerous, that loving someone would get in the way of his duty. He'd have second thoughts about pulling his gun and give some miscreant a split second longer to get the fatal drop on him.

He'd be better off without her. Even though he was falling in love with her.

Falling in love? Hadn't he already fallen? There had been a loud crash Saturday night, when he had seen her across the room.

Mrs. Ghent didn't serve luncheon because a maid took care of that. The cook's responsibilities started with breakfast but the maid did not come in until ten in the morning. When dinner was ready, late in the day, Mrs. Ghent left and the maid served, then cleaned up afterward.

Their days were long during the months the van Roys were in Palm Beach and any other time Pieter and Kiki decided to come to Florida. The rest of the time Mrs. Ghent, who lived with her son, worked with a caterer.

The only reason Cort knew all of this was that he had asked her about it when he found that DePesca was in the neighborhood.

Cort thought it was his duty to know everything that went on in the house when there was some danger afoot. The smallest chink in the armor could be the fatal one.

Cort entered the kitchen after lunch, to explain to Mrs. Ghent that he was at fault for

140

throwing her plans for dinner into disarray.

Mrs. Ghent peered back at him with red-rimmed eyes in her stern face.

"So you see, I want you and the maid out of the house as early as possible tonight," Cort said after he had told her as much as he dared about the possibilities the night hours presented.

"Well, I surely don't care to tangle with who-ever it was that gave you your black eye," Mrs. Ghent snorted. She took a lethal-looking knife from a rack and grasped it firmly. She cleaved a cantaloupe with a single stroke and removed the seeds into a colander with expert scoops of the knife. "I never did believe that story about the boom on the yacht catching."

"I'm only looking out for your welfare," Cort said.

Mrs. Ghent glared at him and reached for the prickly topknot of a pineapple that stood on the butcher block.

"I'll look to my own welfare, as best I can," she proclaimed, laying the pineapple on its side.

"Will you be leaving in your own car, then?"

"Yes."

"What about the maid?"

"She uses the bus."

"That's unacceptable," Cort decided. "I'll have José see her home."

Mrs. Ghent sliced the bottom off the pineapple with a powerful, quick motion. "It's not a problem to get dinner an hour and a half earlier than usual. But it's another matter to have the missus so upset she's talking about going back up north."

She whacked the top off the pineapple and set it aside, then unceremoniously split the fruit into quarters. "I don't blame her for missing her little boy. He's a precious thing, and I miss having him here, too. Last winter was bad enough. Miss Kiki pined for him something fierce, said she wouldn't come back this year without him, but she did."

She rolled a watermelon toward her across the butcher block and studied it for a moment. "In all my years of working here I've never seen a van Roy woman take such a part in raising her young'un. Most haven't had a second thought about leaving their babies to nannies and such. But Miss Kiki, she's a good mother."

"How long have you worked for the van Roys?" Cort asked, his instincts kicking in.

"My father started as their gardener back in '23, and when I turned fourteen in '32, I came to work as a maid. By then my mother was a cook, and my sister worked here, too. We lived over the garage, where your man is stayin'."

Cort felt a surge of hope that she could have a piece to the puzzle of the Roses. "Then maybe you know what happened to—"

"Don't ask me to remember those days," Mrs. Ghent cut him short, aiming her knife at the midsection of the watermelon. "I don't want to tax my memory that much. I've got a fruit salad to make for dinner, and it's some work. See all these seeds?" she asked, using the tip of her sharp knife to indicate the black seeds scattered through the red flesh of the watermelon.

"Yes, ma'am."

"You won't see them in your salad," Mrs. Ghent said firmly and closed him out of any further discussion.

Chapter Seven

At the end of another long, dusty day in the print shop, Jean reached for her time card. She automatically slipped it into the clock to be punched. When she reached to put it in the out slot that had her name on it, Cort's hand clasped hers.

"Hey, you scared me," she gasped, gripping the shoulder strap of her purse reflexively.

"Mr. Evans told me I could wait for you here," Cort explained, pushing himself away from the wall he lounged against. "I didn't want you to walk out of the building by yourself."

She studied his navy blazer, white slacks, and pink knit shirt and marveled at how cool and composed he looked. She noticed the slight lump under his left arm.

"I take it you're carrying your pistol?" she whispered, running a freshly-scrubbed hand over the lapel of his blazer.

His nod was barely perceptible. "Come. Dinner is going to be early tonight."

"Good!" Jean approved, taking his arm. "I get too hungry for dinner at eight."

Cort looked at her and smiled, but she wondered if he really appreciated her attempts to amuse him. There were moments when she wondered if she truly understood him. The difference in the languages they spoke might cause a gulf they could not bridge. Would she be able to learn Dutch well enough to comprehend the nuances of his expressions?

She was willing to try if he was.

Cort exhibited his usual caution at getting her to his car and driving to the mansion. He took a different route than he had the previous evening.

Their attempts at light conversation fell flat. Cort did not seem at all interested in telling her what he had done that day. Nothing she could think of in her day would even slightly interest him.

He was in his own world, scanning the surroundings for danger, concentrating on things that could go wrong. Jean almost wished she didn't have to know anything about it.

The van Roy house was unnaturally quiet when they entered. Only the constant muffled sounds of the waves of the ocean and the barely-distinguishable classical music over the intercom filled the mansion's high-ceilinged rooms.

"I've got to take a shower," Jean told him,

starting toward the curving stairway, feeling almost afraid to touch anything.

Cort shrugged and nodded. "I was hoping we could have a drink together before dinner, but if you think not . . ."

"I'll try to hurry," she promised.

As she reached the top of the stairs, Jean overheard Kiki, talking on the sitting room telephone.

"No, I really do have to cancel, darling," Kiki cooed in an oversweet voice. "I know you think it's frivolous of me to give you such flimsy reasons, but . . . No, of course I love the club's new program. That's not it at all. Oh, dear, I have another call coming in. I hate these phones, don't you? I'll talk to you tomorrow."

Jean paused at the top of the steps, not wanting to let Kiki know that she had heard any of her conversation. But as she took a breath and tried to decide exactly what she should do, Kiki glanced up and saw her. There was no place for Jean to hide.

"Good, you're here." Kiki tugged nervously at the collar of her silk blouse.

Jean mumbled something she hoped sounded cordial. Even though she was tired beyond belief, she was also concerned by the slight puffiness around Kiki's eyes and redness of her nose.

"Did Cort tell you that we're eating early this evening?" Kiki asked, rolling a tissue tightly between her hands.

"Yes, I'll be ready in fifteen minutes," Jean assured her. "Is something wrong?"

Kiki tossed the tissue into a small brass wastebasket near her chair and raised her chin imperiously. "I'm going back to Connecticut. I miss Willie so much," she complained, her voice dangerously close to cracking.

Jean studied Kiki for a long moment, then made a decision that ran contrary to the very fiber of her being. She decided to interfere.

"Can you come to my room for just a moment?" she asked, moving toward the corridor that passed Cort's room. "We need to talk."

Without arguing, Kiki followed her into the small guest room, now cool in the shadows.

Dropping her purse on the top of the writing desk, Jean motioned toward the rocking chair and sat down on the edge of the bed.

"I don't know if you're aware of the gossip going around among your friends," Jean started. "If you can call them friends."

"There's always gossip," Kiki said aloofly, arranging her tissue wool skirt over her crossed knees. "I don't give much credence to it. I think you should just ignore anything you have heard about me."

"I think you should know what was being bandied around the ladies' room at the party Saturday night."

Kiki nodded slightly.

"There's the implication that you have an in-

147

ordinate interest in Cort and that your marriage is—"

"It's not true!" Kiki interrupted hotly. "You're not much better than the busybodies who circulate such rumors if you repeat them to me. Even if you say that you're doing it for my protection. In my best interests. Hah!"

"Frankly, I don't care what you feel about me," Jean told her sincerely. "But you've been kind enough to let me stay in your home at a difficult time. I think I owe you the courtesy of telling you what I heard. I'm also concerned about Cort."

"Still, it's only gossip!"

"I think you should reconsider any action that might make you vulnerable to all sorts of nasty talk, if not something worse. Divorces have been based on less."

"But I want to be with Willie, and I think he needs me," Kiki protested.

"Of course he needs you," Jean stated. "But I think you might talk this over with your husband. See if something could be worked out that would quash the rumors at the same time you get what you want."

Kiki rocked the chair a few times, not taking her eyes off Jean. She made her feel uncomfortable for saying anything at all. Yet Jean did not regret one word of it.

"Yes," Kiki mused. "I could talk Pieter into a week of skiing back home. I miss skiing, you

148

know. At least, that's what we could tell everyone."

"It might be a start," Jean agreed. "I don't know if gossip is as deadly to one's reputation as it used to be. But I'm sure it must make you uncomfortable at the very least. I studied medieval and Renaissance history in college. In those days, socially and politically, a few words of gossip could destroy lives."

"Oh, yes, gossip can be deadly, even now," Kiki confirmed. With a wicked chuckle she got to her feet. "There's a story that I never have fully comprehended about a van Roy man being caught up in some talk back in the twenties. The woman he was supposed to marry nearly did herself in over it. Thank heavens we don't take it that seriously now. Well, I'll get out of your way so you can dress for dinner."

Jean was not entirely happy with the outcome of the conversation. It bothered her that anyone would think she had breached etiquette, even though she had taken that step willingly.

As she showered and dried her hair, she wondered how she could have handled the situation more adroitly. She was distracted from her contemplation by muffled noises from Cort's room and was caught up in thoughts of what he might be doing.

It would be a bittersweet moment when she left this house to go back to her apartment. She had been so quick to take Cort to her heart.

She regretted giving up the little things like hearing his footsteps in the next room, the touch of his hand when she passed him the cream pitcher.

Cort and Pieter were in the library when Jean entered a few minutes later. Like errant schoolboys, they abandoned their conversation the moment they heard her near the door.

Pieter looked extremely tense, but Cort turned to Jean with a practiced smile.

"Would you like something to drink?" Pieter asked her, starting toward the bar.

"No, nothing," Jean said.

Cort shook his head. "It would be best if none of us drinks anything this evening, unless it would be mineral water."

Pieter nodded and set four small green bottles on the bar. Then he dropped ice cubes into three of the crystal glasses lined up on the polished surface. With a flourish he handed filled glasses around.

Jean sipped the mineral water and looked back at Cort. Something that felt very much like fear tightened in her midsection.

"Don't worry," Cort assured her, seeming to read her thoughts. He flexed his fingers on his glass. "Everything will be under control if you just help me a little. It's going to take clear heads and cooperation, though."

Jean took a deep breath. She wished she wasn't wearing high heels for the third night in a row. Cort seemed to expect something to happen tonight, and she just was not prepared.

Kiki had not really changed for dinner. She had added a foulard scarf to her blouse and skirt, and put on more flashy jewelry. Perhaps she didn't want to embarrass Jean as much as she could have.

"Dinner is served," she announced, and grimly led them to the dining room.

Jean sat across the table from Cort. She tried to fit into the family meal unobtrusively and yet not appear to be cowed by the situation.

"From all the data we can come up with, Detective Rolland and I think that DePesca will try to enter this house tonight," Cort said. He unfolded his heavy linen napkin and placed it on his lap. "I'm certain he doesn't know we took the Rose to the bank this morning. According to the officers who were staking out DePesca and Simon, they were eating breakfast at the time. They probably think that the jewelry is in this house. The police have attached a homing device to their boat and to a motor launch at the same dock. We'll get adequate warning when they begin to move, whether by car or boat."

Kiki's fork clattered from her hand onto the bone china plate before her. "I'll just be glad when this is all over," she said, picking up her fork once more.

"Don't worry, Kiki," Pieter assured her, his tone a little more macho than Jean could believe. "I'm here to protect you."

Only Jean saw the flicker of amusement in Cort's eyes. As he turned to hand the salt shaker to Pieter, Jean glimpsed the holster he wore under his jacket.

She didn't think she could eat anything before her, not the fruit salad, the baked chicken, or the asparagus. She forced herself to eat polite amounts of food, but most of her attention was riveted on Cort.

"We are not going to sit here all evening worrying about this man," Cort declared firmly. "But I want you all to try to do what I tell you to do, when I tell you. Don't panic, and don't try to be a hero. If we all work together, the trap will work and no one will get hurt."

"All right," Pieter agreed. "What can we do?"

"Limit your wandering about the house," Cort advised. "Don't leave unnecessary lights on, and stay out of the library."

"Maybe we should all just play a game of bridge in the family room," Kiki proposed, her suggestion trailing off into a nervous giggle.

Jean hoped it wouldn't come to that. She'd never gotten the hang of bridge at college, where students played endless games of it in the commuters' lunchroom, and thought playing cards was a waste of time.

"DePesca does not generally like to encounter

152

people when he enters a house," Cort explained. "When he does, however, he does not leave witnesses. He's always armed, and so is Simon."

"Perhaps we will save the chocolate mousse until later in the evening," Kiki suggested, pushing her chair back. "Does anyone mind?"

"No," Jean mumbled. Chocolate mousse two nights in a row was much too much of a good thing.

"I can't abide these shoes another minute," Jean muttered to Cort as they entered the family room. "Do you mind if I go upstairs and put on some flats?"

"That might be a very good idea," Cort agreed, glancing down at her feet. "Do you want me to come with you?"

"No," Jean said, with a breeziness that was mostly an act. "I've been able to change my own shoes for years."

"It might be fun," he teased, assuring her that he had not missed her attempt to lighten the moment. Then he placed his hand on her arm and kept her close to him for just a moment.

It was long enough that she could feel his warmth and solid substance.

"Be careful," he advised. "Your windows have an excellent view of the seawall. Don't turn on your lights right away, but go to the windows and pull the shades. Stay from between the light and the windows so you don't cast a shadow on them. Then turn out the light and raise the shades again. We may need to use that room as a lookout."

"Now you are frightening me," Jean told him, keeping her voice low so that the others wouldn't hear.

"If you see anything suspicious, don't stand on ceremony," Cort advised, letting her go a few steps away. "Yell."

"But won't they hear me?"

"Not with the waves breaking and the wind blowing," Cort answered. "And what do you think this house is? A biscuit tin?"

Reassured, Jean hurried to her room and followed Cort's instructions to the letter. As she neared the windows to draw the shades, she looked out at the ocean. But she saw nothing near or on its black surface that should not have been there.

When she was finished and raised one of the shades, she saw a man pulling himself up over the seawall.

Not bothering to raise the other shade, Jean ran from the room and flew down the stairs.

"Cort! You were right!" Jean called from the hallway, not waiting to reach the room. "There's a man down by the water."

"I wonder how he got past the police," Cort mused calmly, hurrying to meet her at the bottom of the steps.

154

Pieter and Kiki followed him from the family room and looked to him for instructions.

"José isn't back from seeing the maid home, so, Kiki, you'll have to take his station. Go to the front door and watch for the police cars to draw up, then open the gate. Don't do it too soon, or DePesca will see the gate open and know we are on to him."

"How will I know when to open the gate, then?" Kiki asked.

"I guess you'll have to rely on your best judgment," Cort told her.

Kiki nodded grimly, touched Pieter's arm briefly, and went to take up her post.

Just then the telephone rang.

"That will be the police," Cort said. "Pieter, tell them we're ready."

Pieter hurried away toward the family room.

"Come with me," Cort ordered, pushing Jean ahead of him.

But Jean held back, conscious of Cort taking off his jacket as he walked.

He tossed it aside onto a nearby chair. "I want you to stay clear of the library. Just sit in the family room."

"Won't you need me as a witness?"

"No. I need you to be out of harm's way."

Cort almost pushed her into the family room, then paused to check that his pistol was loaded. "Piet, you stay here, too," Cort ordered, without diverting his attention from his pistol.

Jean glanced around the room, startled. Pieter van Roy was not there. At the far side of the room a cabinet was opened, and the lid of a felt-lined pistol case stood raised.

"Cort!" Jean called, her voice soft but urgent, trying to bring Pieter's absence to his attention. But Cort was moving out of the room, along the corridor that led back to the library.

Intent on letting Cort know that Pieter was somewhere other than where he was supposed to be, Jean followed.

Cort drew in a deep breath and took stock of the situation. The hallway was darkened to reduce the intruders' ability to get around in the unfamiliar house. Cort didn't think for a moment that DePesca did not case his victims' homes. He'd been known to pay a municipal clerk to provide plans to see how the house was laid out.

It took a moment for his eyes to adjust to the darkness and his ears to the sounds—the ticking of a clock, the pounding of the ocean waves beyond the walls.

His pistol was solid and steady in his hand, but this time it was little comfort. He didn't dare follow the niggling thought he had in the back of his mind. It would make him want to turn around and go back to the family room to check that Pieter and Jean were all right. The weakest link in the equation, Kiki, was out of the way just where he wanted her, far away from the action.

He neared the door of the library, moving close to the wall for the cover it afforded. Cort heard what could have been bushes rustling or a foot scraping on the stone patio outside the library doors. DePesca would not make a noise, but Simon—if Jean's roommate Denise's observation was valid—had put on weight. He might not be as agile as he used to be.

Maybe in Cort's attempt to hear something, he was amplifying the casual sounds of the wind in his mind.

He flexed his fingers on his pistol. At the same time he heard a footfall on the hall carpet behind him and felt a presence. He took a breath and smelled Jean's scent, powder and soap and light, sweet spices.

"Cort," Jean whispered to him, "Pieter isn't in the family room, and I think he's got a gun."

"Damn!" Cort swore beneath his breath without looking back at her. He didn't blame Pieter for wanting to defend his home, his wife, and his own life. But Pieter had picked a poor time to be brave.

In a heartbeat Cort reviewed all the times he and his cousin had engaged in a comradely rivalry, Cort usually getting the best of it. Damn! It was the worst possible time for Pieter to try to outdo him.

God! Where the hell was Pieter?

A latch gave and a hinge creaked ever so softly. He hoped Pieter could be patient enough to let DePesca get to work on the safe before making a move.

"Stay here," Cort hissed at Jean.

Whether she answered or not, he was not sure. The way things had been going lately, he could not even count on her cooperation.

Cort peered into the darkened library and saw the point of light from a flashlight searching for the wall safe. He felt a breeze from the door, left open for the escape.

He slipped his hand into the room and reached toward the light switch. But before he could flip the switch, the room was bathed in light from the chandelier—probably Pieter's going from the other entrance to the room.

There was a loud curse that Cort did not bother to translate to the language he was thinking in at the moment. He moved forward, lowering himself into a half-crouching stance.

"Stop right there!" Pieter commanded, his voice firm at first, then almost cracking in fear.

Now in the library himself, Cort studied the situation. Both DePesca and Simon had guns, and DePesca drew his, perhaps not seeing Cort, blinded still by the sudden light.

But a shot deafened Cort for an instant, sending the crystals of the chandelier into a nervous chiming from the report.

Pieter slumped to the floor.

"Drop it, Stefano!" Cort yelled. "You, too, Simon. Pieter! Are you all right?"

Jean entered the room and hurried to Pieter's aid. "It's his upper arm," she assessed, and Cort took comfort in her calm appraisal.

Pistol drawn, one policeman slipped in the door Stefano had left ajar, and was followed by others. Kiki led the local detective in from the hallway.

Glancing around to see that everything was under control, Cort slipped the safety back on his pistol and returned it to his holster.

Damn! Why was it that at the moment he should be feeling exhilaration at catching the man he'd been after for so long, he was going into a cold sweat?

Several police officers scattered around the room to handcuff the thieves. They recited the necessary legal cautions before removing them to awaiting squad cars.

"They're all yours," Cort told the detectives.

Then he heard the ripping of cloth behind him. He turned to see what Jean was doing for Pieter, and suddenly felt a chill of apprehension at the sight of blood.

Jean had ripped the sleeve of Pieter's shirt away from his upper arm.

"Do you need any help there, Jean?" Cort asked, moving backward a few steps and dividing his attention between the two cen-

159

ters of activity in the room.

"Get this gun out of my way," she demanded tightly, nodding her head toward Pieter's pistol, which lay on the carpet at her knee.

Before Cort could oblige, one of the policemen moved toward her. "I'll take care of that," he offered, picking it up and quickly removing the bullets. He handed the gun to José, who had just arrived in the room, breathless and apologetic.

"The slug is still in the wound," Jean informed him. She glanced up at the distraught Kiki. "I need some towels."

"Right!" Kiki snapped and turned away.

But José motioned for her to stay where she was and hurried out of the library.

Pieter grimaced. "It hurts," he said slowly. Kiki grabbed a throw pillow from a nearby chair and placed it under his head, gently stroking Pieter's hair from his forehead.

"I'll call for an ambulance," Detective Rolland said, reaching for the field phone that was clipped to his belt.

"What can I do?" Cort asked Jean, dropping to crouch beside his cousin.

"Hold his hand," Jean suggested, applying pressure to Pieter's wound.

Cort wrapped his fingers around Pieter's and felt for his pulse with his other hand. It was fast but strong.

A look passed between them. Pieter was

vaguely apologetic, his eyes showing his pain, his face pale.

"I . . . I wanted to help," Pieter mumbled.

"All's well that ends well," Cort quoted, and felt Pieter's pulse slow perceptibly.

Cort was impressed by how capably Jean had handled the situation. Her slender hand was clamped firmly over the wound, the faintest traces of blood showing between her fingers.

José hurried into the library and shoved a handful of white kitchen towels at Jean. "Are these all right?"

"Fine," Jean told him. "Fold one really small — good!"

As Jean took the prepared towel, Cort saw the blood on her palm and fought down a twinge of queasiness.

But Jean never flinched, applying the towel to the wound and asking Kiki to rip a strip of fabric from Pieter's torn shirtsleeve to secure it with.

"Cort, will you come with us to the station and help with the paperwork?" Rolland asked, tapping him on the shoulder.

For the first time in his professional life Cort hesitated. He wanted to stay with Pieter, to comfort Kiki, to hold on to Jean for reassurance.

But he got to his feet slowly. "Piet, hang in there and I'll see you in a little while. Captain, I'll have my man drive me downtown."

He touched Jean's shoulder briefly to assure her that he admired her strength through all of this. She truly had proven herself to be exceptional.

The emergency service attendants assured Kiki that Pieter was in no danger once the bleeding had stopped. He would have to be taken to the hospital, however.

Kiki insisted that Jean come with them in the ambulance, then hurried away. When she returned with her purse and coat, she fretted about having the right insurance cards and identification.

The attendant who monitored Pieter's condition seemed to understand the temperament of a woman like Kiki.

Jean had no wish to be left behind at the house. If Kiki wanted her for emotional support, she would be there.

Kiki returned to the waiting area from the task of filling out papers and sagged into one of the sturdy chairs.

"Don't you always feel like such a dunce when you have to go through something like this?" Kiki asked. "They made me feel as though I shot Pieter. And it's worse if Willie gets hurt. I feel as though I'm being accused of something horrible. I never get a scratch, but I think the two of them are accident-prone. That's another reason I don't like being away from Willie."

Jean reached out and put her hand on Kiki's arm. "Pieter will be all right," she said.

"Of course he will be. I can't thank you enough." Kiki put her hand over Jean's. "Oh, look. Blood on your dress. Send me the bill when you have it cleaned."

"I'll just wash it in cold-water soap," Jean told her. "It'll be all right."

It was her best dress, maybe ruined. Her very best dress. Maybe she would send it to a cleaners and send Kiki the bill, if she found the nerve. It should only matter that Pieter would be all right.

Kiki pressed her lips together firmly, making a rather unattractive face. Jean knew she was fighting hard to keep her composure.

"You remember what we talked about before dinner?" she asked, but went on without waiting for an answer. "Things like this put your life into perspective. I . . . I don't know if I could face life without Pieter. Do you know what I mean?"

Jean nodded.

"I hope Pieter doesn't have any doubts about my devotion to him," Kiki whispered painfully. "I certainly don't. Not anymore."

Jean smiled at her. "Good."

It was a telephone call Cort had been anxious

to make. Now he dreaded hearing Robert's voice on the other end of the line. He perched on the corner of Rolland's desk and waited for the overseas connection.

"I hope you have something worthwhile to tell me," Robert growled.

Cort glanced at his watch to see what time it was in Paris. Cort came straight to the point. "We have DePesca and Simon in custody."

"Well done. How much mischief did they get into?"

"My cousin Pieter took a bullet."

"How bad?"

"It didn't look too bad." Cort took a deep breath.

"Italy came through with extradition orders, so as soon as they are messengered to Palm Beach, I want you to—"

"Robert, this was my holiday!" Cort objected, getting to his feet. "I've spent nearly my whole week on this stupid case."

"No, you haven't," Robert argued, then laughed. "You've spent part of the time chasing that pretty blonde with green eyes."

"I've got better things to do than accompany DePesca back to Italy. Let some fine Italian deputy take over."

"Oh, all right. Can you tear yourself away to be back in Paris next Monday?"

"Make it Wednesday," Cort countered, always one to test the limits.

"Tuesday," Robert ordered wearily.

Cort hung up the telephone and looked down at the papers Rolland's stenographer had handed him for his signature. "The papers are being messengered from Rome," he told Rolland. "Do you need me for anything more?"

"No. Nice doing business with you, Cort."

They shook hands and Cort strode out of the office, not pausing until he got to his car in the parking lot. He should have told Robert that he could not possibly continue as an investigator. But he felt as though his life had ended and he was going to have to think about it for a long while.

José drove him to the hospital, where he found Pieter about to be released.

Kiki was pale and flustered but in somewhat calmer condition than she had been earlier. Jean was helping them keep their composure with her businesslike attitude.

"No tennis for a while," Pieter muttered glumly as Cort helped him into the front seat of the car. "I suppose you're angry with me."

"Yes, I am," Cort said, "but I'm so glad to have this case wrapped up that I don't feel it."

In the brief moment that they waited for Kiki to get into the back seat of the car, Jean slipped her hand into Cort's. Their fingers intertwined. It was a gesture of mutual forgiveness for causing each other all the trouble they had been through, as well as congratulations on jobs well-done. But most of all, that clasp of hands was a celebration of spirits joined in a profound communion.

Chapter Eight

Kiki tucked her leather coat closer to her and settled her shoulders against the seat. "The season is a disaster, anyway," she groused. "We may as well both go home."

"Please, Kiki," Pieter complained, "I'm in no mood to argue."

Kiki, however, was in a mood to say everything she had been holding back. Jean felt deeply embarrassed to be trapped in the back seat of the car, forced to listen to what should have been a very private discussion.

In her discomfort Jean looked up at Cort, close beside her. She saw in the darkness that he was as uncomfortable as she was. He shook his head in silent apology, then stared out the window at the streetlights they passed.

When they reached the house, Cort quickly whisked Pieter up the curving stairway. Kiki hurried after them, suddenly solicitous and wifely.

"I'll make us some coffee," Jean called after

them.

"Warm milk," Cort suggested.

"Mrs. Ghent would make hot chocolate," Kiki said, coming back down a few steps. "I think we'd all like that better."

Jean went into the kitchen and began searching for a saucepan and cocoa powder. She expected to find some exotic versions of basic staples when she chanced on packets of mix that made hot chocolate when added to boiled water.

"Why, Mrs. Ghent, you old fraud!" she exclaimed. Laughing, Jean took the box from the shelf and held it up to read the directions.

Behind her, she heard some shuffling noises outside the door and the scraping of a key in the lock. Mrs. Ghent let herself into the kitchen and stopped cold to see Jean standing there.

"So," Mrs. Ghent said, as though demanding an explanation of Jean's presence in her territory.

"I was just going to make some—"

"How's Mr. van Roy?" Mrs. Ghent asked, waving aside the statement of the obvious to get to more important matters. "I heard the call for an ambulance on my son's police scanner."

"Pieter will be fine," Jean assured her. "It was merely a wound to his upper arm."

"Lord! I thought it would have been Mr. Cort!" Mrs. Ghent exclaimed, snatching the box from Jean's hand and turning on the element under the teakettle. "How did Mr. Pieter get mixed up in all of this?"

Jean, effectively shouldered out of doing anything, recounted the events of the evening for the cook.

"Well, a fine kettle of fish," Mrs. Ghent snorted, taking a cocoa set from the china cupboard. "I suppose Miss Kiki will be even more determined to go back up North."

Her tone gave Jean a definite clue to what Mrs. Ghent thought of this change in plans.

"I'm afraid so." Jean sighed. She understood that Mrs. Ghent was not likely to get paid for work she didn't do. Knowing a little about the plight of the elderly in Florida, Jean wondered what financial support the old woman had.

Jean was about to ask Mrs. Ghent how long she had been working for the family when Cort entered the kitchen.

Mrs. Ghent made a dismissing motion toward him, but he did not back out the door.

"We'll take the chocolate to the upstairs parlor," he said. "I want to build a fire, but there's no kindling up there, Mrs. Ghent."

"There's plenty in the shed by the garage," Mrs. Ghent told him. "Put a sweater on or you'll catch cold," she advised, raising her voice as he headed out of the kitchen. "I swear, he's as much trouble as any of 'em."

Amused, Jean hoped some anecdote would

169

follow so that she could judge how long Mrs. Ghent had worked for the family, but the cook turned to giving orders.

"There are biscuits in that tin over there," Mrs. Ghent pointed out. "They call them biscuits; I call them cookies."

"They look delicious," Jean complimented, taking the top off the tin.

"They're not for looking at," Mrs. Ghent snorted. "Take a couple to try on the way upstairs, then you can put on polite airs and turn down the last one you're offered."

Jean felt that Mrs. Ghent had accepted her as a friend, a person she could trust with her eccentric and wry assessment of the family who employed her. She wished she could press that slight advantage to talk about what the cook might know of the early days of the van Roys' life in Palm Beach. But perhaps this camaraderie was too new to exploit. Jean decided not to push.

Mrs. Ghent could not be talked out of taking the tray upstairs. The sitting room was a comfortable wide place at the top of the stairs with a small raised hearth and several cushy chairs. Jean reasoned that the cook probably wanted to get a glimpse of Pieter to see that he was indeed still among the living, although uncomfortable.

"He's already taken a pain pill and gone to bed," Kiki told the woman when she was asked

170

how Pieter was. "Good night, Mrs. Ghent."

When the cook had lumbered back down the stairs, Kiki picked up her cup and settled into a chair with a weary sigh. "That woman can be the biggest busybody! Of course, she's been with the family forever, so we can't fire her."

"Why would you want to?" Cort asked, closing the screen in front of the fire and brushing his hands together. "She's a marvelous cook."

"Yes, of course," Kiki agreed. "But it costs us something each month to retain her so we'll have someone to take care of us in case we come down here on a whim. I sometimes think she's too old to be hovering over us the way she does."

"I think she likes to hover," Cort observed. "It's probably what keeps her going."

"It's not our place to worry about things like that," Kiki explained, frustration evident in her voice. "At least, it's not supposed to be. I'm not used to all of this, you know, Jean. Since I married Pieter, I've tried to fit in with all the habits that were already set up. Now that Pieter's parents are gone and we have to carry on their traditions, it seems like a lot of nonsense.

Cort looked down at her with raised eyebrows, then he glanced over at Jean. They both seemed to have realized that there was a depth to Kiki they had not seen before the events of the last few hours.

Abruptly Kiki put her cup down on the table

171

beside her chair. "I hope you two don't mind," she apologized, getting to her feet. "But I'm very poor company tonight. I'd much rather go see that Pieter is sleeping comfortably and stay with him."

"I understand," Jean assured her, knowing that her being there had put a strain on Kiki. "I certainly don't need to be entertained. I don't think I'll stay up much longer myself."

Kiki left the room with a swirl of her soft wool skirt. A moment later there was the muffled clicking of the door to the master suite. The silence of the sitting room was punctuated by the crackling of the fire.

Jean absorbed the scene of Cort standing with his foot braced on the hearth. He used an iron poker to position a log over the center of the fire, while his other hand held the delicate cocoa cup.

He was not wearing his pistol.

Satisfied that the fire would burn a while longer, Cort closed the screen and turned to Jean.

"I think this is my favorite room in the whole world," he mused, as he pushed a footstool toward her chair with his knee. "I tried to make a room like this in my home, but there is something not quite right."

Jean watched as he folded himself onto the stool at her knees. He refilled her cup, then drained the pot into his own.

172

"I think what is missing is a certain touch," he observed slowly. "A woman's touch, perhaps. Somehow women know what makes a place comfortable. I think you would."

Jean laughed, feeling the warmth of the hot chocolate in her cup flowing through her fingers. "What makes you think that?" she asked him.

"You have style. I've found that it is the least of your virtues." His eyes turned very serious. "Tonight I saw in you a strength in adversity that I admire more than you can know. When you were taking care of Pieter, you turned your back to DePesca and Simon. You didn't seem afraid of his wound."

"I knew you had your gun trained on DePesca and Simon, and I knew Pieter was not mortally wounded," Jean told him, then shrugged. "I had nothing to lose."

"You had a lot to lose the moment you entered that room," Cort told her. He knotted his hands around the cocoa cup. Jean saw the strength of his anguish in the way his fingers dug into each other. "What if I tried to shoot and my gun jammed? It would have been another picture."

"I don't waste much time on thinking about what might have been," Jean said, reaching out to place her hand on his. "It all worked out the way it did. It's over."

"Only the worst part—the trap to snare De-

Pesca—is over, Jean," he murmured. "There is so much between us that is a mystery. It must be solved before we can move on, whether we are together or separate. We must find out how you came to own the Champagne Rose."

She could see that what he wanted to say was not coming easily. She wondered if he couldn't find the right word and translate it to English, or if the concept was in itself difficult.

With a look of apology Cort moved his hands from her grasp. He took a long swallow of hot chocolate and put the cup aside on the table.

"Has it ever occurred to you that you might be a cousin to us?" he asked, a darkly-troubled look in his eyes.

Jean stared at him until the liquid in her cup almost spilled. "What a stupid thought!"

"Listen, darling, not all the van Roy sons were perfect angels," he told her. "There were two in the house here in 1925—my grandfather and Pieter's. One of them could have seduced your great-grandmother. I shudder to think that it might have been mine, but if such a thing occurred, it was more likely Pieter's. My grandfather always told me that the Champagne Rose was not stolen as everyone claimed."

"I don't want to hear another word of this," Jean stated flatly. She would have stood and run to her room had not Cort been in her way.

"I would prefer to save my breath, too, and

174

never think of the possibility again," he told her. "If I did not care for you, if I didn't love you, it wouldn't matter to me. But I do love you, and therefore, I must know."

"Let me see if I understand you," Jean said. "You think someone from your family seduced my great-grandmother and gave her the Champagne Rose to buy her silence."

Cort closed his eyes wearily and nodded. "It sounds terrible and fantastic, but it's the only way I can make sense of it."

"How are we ever going to know?" Jean asked, feeling a sickness in the pit of her stomach.

"Would you go back to your hometown and look at the records? Find out when your great-grandmother's first child was born and if you are descended from that person?"

"When?"

"Right away. I must know!"

"Don't be silly!" Jean scoffed. "It's winter there."

"Jean, it's important to me—to us!"

"Cort, no. I can see that it's important, but can't it wait until April, when the snow is gone?"

"No," he answered, taking away her cup and clutching both her hands in his. "Every day, every hour, I am more in love with you. If we must turn our backs on each other because we are related by blood, it must be now, before such a situation would ruin our lives forever."

"What would we be? Second cousins?" Jean speculated. "That isn't . . . bad—"

"In my family's circumstances it would not be acceptable," he stated bluntly. He paused as though he might have said more, but he must have decided against it. "Jean, please . . ."

"Cort, it's a lot to ask, just to satisfy your curiosity," Jean argued desperately. "I work for a living, and I don't have the money to just drop everything and run up home. I don't have a car, and to take a bus would be agony. To fly would be out of the question. I honestly don't have the money, and I don't think Ben Evans would hold my job until I got back."

Cort's head drooped and she studied the way his dark hair fell in broad black feathers from its part. She wanted to free her hands so she could touch it, but he held her hands tightly in the warmth of his.

"I'll work on that, on getting your money," he promised at last. He let go of her hands and got to his feet. "I'm flying to London Wednesday night, and from there to Antwerp. So on your lunchtime Wednesday we'll have to go to the bank and get the Champagne Rose. I have already talked to a contact at an auction house there. He can add the Champagne Rose to a gem auction being held a week from tomorrow. You have until Wednesday noon to change your mind about selling."

"No, I won't change my mind," Jean informed him. "I don't want to sell it, but I have no choice, do I?"

"My friend is sending papers to be signed via a fax machine at the police station. I'll hand-deliver them with the jewel. The papers will be in Dutch, but I'll translate it all for you."

Jean started to get to her feet, and Cort pulled her into his arms.

"It will be a very sad goodbye for us," he said, holding her close. "Especially if you find out what I am afraid of."

"I wish you didn't have to leave," she complained, allowing her cheek to press against his. "I wish that everything could stay just the way it is now."

"But if I leave, and take your diamond to be auctioned, you could be a wealthy woman," Cort said, looking down at her.

"You haven't learned the first thing about me," Jean sighed. "Money is not the most important thing in my life."

"What is?" he asked.

"Before Saturday night?" she asked. "Seeing what I can of the world and helping people who need help."

"And since Saturday night?" he asked softly, his lips very close to hers.

"I think . . . you already . . . know."

It was an irresistible kiss, filled with all the frustrations and hardships of the day. They shared the longings they both felt and the constraints in which they found themselves. It was sweeter for being vaguely forbidden, more powerful for being so very tender.

Reluctantly Jean drew away from Cort, knowing that she had to preserve some dignity. If she told him that she loved him, he would insist on more intimacy, and she was not prepared for that.

Before Jean understood what Cort was doing, he had pushed the footstool aside. He sagged into the chair she had been sitting in and pulled her onto his lap. He cradled her to him and pressed his lips to her cheek.

Perhaps this would be the last time they could be together like this, she thought. If that was so, she would make the most of it.

Cort reached out to turn off the lamp that stood on the table beside them. Only the light from the fire on the hearth illuminated the room.

It was more than the fire's heat that warmed her. There was no doubt in her mind that Cort desired her as much as she longed to give herself to him. And that was an insanity she fought against with all her moral strength. Hers was not a character of easy virtue.

Time lost all meaning, and whether they sat together for a minute or an hour, Jean couldn't tell.

Her hand rested on his shoulder, where she

could feel his warmth and strength, and she did not want to leave him. With great reluctance she kissed his cheek, on the long vertical line that made his smile so devastating.

"Tomorrow will come very quickly," she sighed.

"Yes," he whispered, catching her hand in his and holding it close to his mouth. Without breaking the heated gaze with which he captured her eyes, he pressed a kiss onto her palm.

"I should be going to my room."

"So should I," Cort agreed but didn't move a muscle.

The fire in the hearth died to a few embers before Jean pulled herself from Cort's embrace.

"Good night, my darling," he said, letting her go.

At the corner of the room, where it became the corridor that led to their rooms, Jean turned and looked back at Cort.

He had not left the chair but gazed grimly at the fire.

Ben Evans had an annoyed look on his face when he motioned for Jean to pick up the extension phone nearest her. She sighed and put down her half-finished can of soda. She was, after all, on her break. She'd rather not have to deal with someone making a last-minute change

179

in an ad layout.

"Barbour here," she answered, adding yet another smudge to the receiver of the phone.

"Darling," Cort said. The noise behind him led her to believe that he was not at the mansion.

"Cort?" Jean asked. "What's up?"

Cort chuckled. "Stefano DePesca, and Simon, at about thirty thousand feet, on their way to Rome, even as we speak." He was almost breathless with elation.

"Really?"

"You know what that means?"

"Denise and I can go back to the apartment."

"Denise can go back to the apartment. Stay one more night with us?" he pleaded.

"It's tempting, Cort," she told him. "Perhaps too much so. But Denise and I have to get back to normal."

"Think about it. I'll see you at five."

When she had broken the connection, she called Denise at the boutique where she worked.

"The coast is clear," she announced. "We can go back to the apartment."

"Great!" Denise responded. "Hey, things are slow here today. I can meet you for lunch at Freeman's Deli."

"Hmm! Twelve-thirty?" Jean asked.

"You have a lot of explaining to do, girl."

"Do I ever!" Jean laughed, then smiled at Ben, who was giving her a sternly-reproving glare.

They had eaten in Freeman's so often that Denise and Jean knew the menu by heart. But Jean still had to count her money, deciding what she would need between now and payday on Friday.

Did she dare splurge? She had been eating pretty well lately, all the rich food. She debated between several items, and then ordered her usual.

Joey put a salad plate in front of Jean and a tuna sandwich in front of Denise. Then he stood by silently while Jean took Denise's dill pickle and Denise filched Jean's sliced tomato.

"I love watching you do that," he teased.

"The show's over, kid," Denise told him with a flash of her dark eyes and a dismissing gesture. "We have serious girl-talk to do here."

"Enjoy," Joey said cheerfully, wiping his hands on his apron and moving to another table to take an order.

"So, tell me all about Mr. International Gorgeous Sleuth," Denise ordered, squeezing a slice of lemon into her iced tea.

"You've seen him. You know he's fantastic."

"To look at, sure, but—"

They were interrupted by someone approaching the table from the deli counter. Jean looked up and stifled a groan.

The woman Jean had encountered twice at the hotel tried to start a conversation. "I hear there was a lot of excitement at the van Roy's last night." She carried a paper sack from which protruded the end of a loaf of Freeman's seeded rye.

"Yes," Jean replied, putting her fork aside before she could attack her potato salad with the vigor she'd like to assert on the person interrupting.

"Were you there at the time?" she asked casually.

"Yes," Jean answered hesitantly.

"Did you actually see the jewel thieves?" she asked with growing interest.

Jean nodded, wishing she could get to her lunch. She was reminded of the conversation she'd had with Kiki the day before. She owed Kiki the favor of derailing any mischief the woman could engineer.

"How badly was Pieter van Roy hurt?" the woman wanted to know, her eyes widening at the chance to collect a juicy tidbit of gossip.

"I believe he's canceled his tennis game for today," Jean stated coolly.

"And how is Kiki?" the woman pried.

"I haven't seen her today, but she was very upset last night until she knew Pieter would be all right," Jean said, hoping that morsel would satisfy the woman's curiosity.

"And Cort van Roy?"

"Will be leaving for Europe tomorrow evening," Jean supplied, her tone closing the subject.

"Will you be going with him?"

Jean laughed, more at the woman's nerve in asking than at the preposterous supposition she was making. "No," she replied, regaining her composure. "I have too many obligations here."

"I wish I could stay and chat longer," the woman said, "but I have some friends coming for luncheon at one. Toodles."

Denise could barely contain herself until the door had closed behind the woman.

"Sorry she had to leave so soon!" Denise exclaimed, selecting a potato chip from the pile on her plate. "What happened last night?"

"DePesca and Simon broke into van Roys' to rob the safe, Pieter surprised them a little more than Cort wanted them to be surprised, and Pieter was shot."

"God!" Denise breathed and crossed herself.

"Just in the arm," Jean went on. "He'll be fine in a few weeks. Now, may I eat?"

"As though the van Roys starved you," Denise teased. "Come on, what did you eat?"

"Chicken, fruit," Jean told her, finally free to attack her potato salad. "So what's new? Their cook is a strange old woman, looks old as dirt. She's a good cook and fixes lovely food. But I opened her cupboard, and you know what I found?"

Denise leaned forward, hanging on Jean's every word. "What?"

"Mixes!" Jean divulged. "Expensive ones, but mixes."

Denise laughed. "So, is it serious between you and Cort?"

"Give me a break! I just met him Saturday night—"

"Hey, I see this look in your eyes," Denise told her. "With other women, it's love. Tell me it's not."

"He's very attractive, very attentive, very . . . continental," Jean explained. "He plans to take the Champagne Rose to Antwerp to be auctioned." She paused to take a bite of her pickle.

"And split the money with you?" Denise scoffed. "Or just split, period?"

"We hadn't really discussed his getting anything out of it."

Denise chuckled, a touch of irony in her tone. "I didn't think the turnip truck stopped by here anymore! Jean, how can you be so stupid? I don't care if he is Interpol. I don't care if he's St. Francis. You wave a million dollars at someone and see how fast they can be corrupted, and how fast they can be out of sight. Gone. Forever. Jean, Jean, Jean!"

"Are you through?" Jean asked after a moment.

"Yes, and so are you."

"Look, to me the Champagne Rose is just a piece of pretty glass. If he wants it, he can have it. If he's a con man, I'm really no worse off now than I was before."

"Yes, you are, if you love him." Denise leaned back in her chair, preparing to be instructive. "If you haven't already known it, there are men who take great satisfaction in humiliating women. He could be that way and still be what he says he is."

"No!" Jean defended. "Not Cort! Maybe I love him. Maybe he is going to cheat me, but so far, I haven't lost anything—I repeat anything—that I hold very dear. If I never see him again, I'll certainly be disappointed, but I'll survive."

"Sure, and I have some property I'd like to sell you."

Jean stared at Denise for a long moment, thinking that Cort had said that very thing to her. It implied hopeless naivete on her part, and perhaps they were both right. If she didn't take this risk, she'd never know the Champagne Rose's value or if Cort was all she hoped he was.

The silence between them was uncomfortable for a moment. It was not a novel experience. Denise had a definite outlook on the world in general. Jean found that the best way of living with Denise was to keep her ideas to herself.

It had to do with Jean's concept of the

proper order of things. She had asked to live with Denise; therefore, she adapted to Denise's lifestyle and philosophy. If she could not be accommodating, she kept her peace and went along with Denise as far as was prudent.

Denise touched her napkin to the corners of her mouth and pointed her fork at Jean. "But on the other hand, what would you do if he really came through for you?"

Jean stared at her roommate for a long moment. There was no accounting for the way Denise could switch gears conversationally.

"I have no idea," Jean said. "I haven't given it a moment's thought."

"How could you avoid it?"

"Oh, all right! I thought of opening my own boutique, but that's more something you would do. There are not a lot of things a student of Renaissance history can do to make a living on the open market," Jean explained thoughtfully. "I could go back to school and get my doctorate, maybe teach, and have a little money put by to fill in the lean spots."

Denise studied Jean with skepticism in her eyes, but she kept what she was thinking to herself.

Cort was waiting for Jean again that afternoon when she finished at the print shop.

"I could get very used to this," Jean said

with a laugh. She tied the sleeves of her Irish knit pullover around her neck and slipped her arm around Cort's lean waist.

"So could I," he agreed, resting his hand possessively on her shoulder and kissing her.

She looked up at him in surprise. "In public! I'm shocked."

"Wait until you see Paris." He chuckled, leading her to his car. "Paris is for lovers. You can't help seeing it. I can imagine us riding on a boat on the Seine at twilight on a warm spring evening . . ."

Jean laughed. "I'm too busy to imagine anything right now," she said. "I just have to get all my things from van Roys' and help Denise get the apartment back in order."

"I feel slighted," Cort complained playfully. "You can't spare even a thought for me."

Jean leaned against the supple leather of the car seat and rested her head. If he only knew how many times that day she'd had to push him out of her consciousness! How many times his handsome face had intruded between her and her work! He would have felt anything but slighted.

"Your eye is much better," Jean appraised.

"Thank you. So is the lump on my lip," Cort said, putting the car in gear. "I'm glad you can find something good to say to me."

Just when Jean thought she had insulted him, Cort began to laugh. He reached out to take her hand and kissed her fingers without taking his eyes from the street ahead of him.

At the house Jean sensed an electricity, a flurry of activity that she had not known before. It was usually a quiet place, with only the waves outside and muffled classical music giving any sustained sound.

But a phone was ringing, and hurried footfalls echoed through the rooms. There were even snatches of quiet conversation.

In the pleasant room she had used, Jean collected her belongings, packed her suit and dress into her garment bag, and checked all the drawers to see if she had left anything behind.

"What on earth are you doing?" Kiki demanded as Jean was about to strip her bed.

Jean froze, her hands clutching the bedspread. "I thought I'd take the sheets off so the maid—"

"Don't bother, Jean." Kiki fluttered her hands. "We're leaving tomorrow, so she can do everything at one time."

"You're leaving?" Jean asked.

"We've decided to fly home," Kiki told her, entering the room and glancing out the windows at the ocean. "It's the perfect solution to everything, don't you see? Pieter really wants to see his own doctor about his arm, and I miss Willie. And Cort's leaving, anyway."

"Yes, I know."

"We had to hire a pilot, since Pieter is hurt," Kiki went on. "We wanted Cort to fly the plane, but he'd already made plans to go on a commercial flight. His time is tightly scheduled so he can take care of that business for you before he goes back to Paris. We thought we'd drop you off in Pennsylvania. Cort said you had some records to check into."

"He takes a lot for granted! I can't just pick up and leave my job," Jean complained, suddenly angry that Cort had made plans behind her back.

She wasn't surprised, though. His penchant for taking charge of dangerous situations would naturally extend to taking over every situation. She'd heard that European men were that way. Suddenly the romance had fallen flat.

"Oh," Kiki said. "I thought you'd talked this over."

"No, we hadn't," Jean stated a little more forcefully than she'd intended. Then she reined in her emotions and took a deep breath. "I'm sorry. This has nothing to do with you. I guess these things happen when . . . when—"

"When you're starting a new relationship and you don't know each other's ways and feelings very well?" Kiki asked. "Yes, I'd say he should have discussed it with you."

"In a way, I guess he did," Jean admitted, feeling deflated. "I don't know if I agreed to go home and look things up. I certainly didn't mean that I would do it right away. Maybe after the weather turns nice there. I certainly can't go on such short notice. I don't have the money, and I don't even have a winter coat anymore. I gave mine to someone who had to make an emergency trip to Virginia, and I can't very well ask her to give it back."

"Is that all you're worried about?" Kiki asked.

"Job, money, coat," Jean ticked off. "That's about it, and I think it's plenty."

"Your boss will probably hold your job for a little while, won't he?" Kiki asked. "I only worked for a year, but I recall people sometimes had emergencies."

"Maybe," Jean conceded, zipping her duffel bag closed. "But you don't know Ben Evans."

"We're giving you the plane ride home," Kiki pointed out. "As for a coat, I'll loan you one of mine and you can mail it back to me."

Jean stared at Kiki. When she had met the woman, she hadn't thought she had a practical or generous thought in her head. Obviously she had underestimated her.

Cort strode into the room, followed by José, who silently picked up Jean's bags and left with them.

"I have some papers for you to sign," he told Jean. "Could we go down to the library where there are dictionaries to help me explain—"

"Yes, you do have some explaining to do,"

Jean told him firmly. "Kiki, thank you for your offers. I'll think about what you said and get back to you later."

"Something's wrong," Cort observed as they started down the curving stairway to the main floor.

"You seem to have made a lot of plans without my knowledge," Jean observed. "And I certainly don't like being talked about out of my presence."

"I'm very sorry about that," Cort apologized. "I didn't know that you'd mind."

"I can't just drop everything, go home, and poke around in records that I don't even know will yield what we want to know," Jean contended. "And I don't want to inconvenience your cousins any further. Staying here two nights was certainly enough."

Chapter Nine

Cort led her into the library and dropped the papers he was holding onto the polished oak table. "Are you finished lecturing me?" he demanded.

"Probably not," Jean replied, sitting down abruptly in one of the leather chairs.

Cort frowned, his black brows coming together over his gray eyes. "I'm sorry. I didn't know that you would be so upset. But I must make some decisions quickly, and to make them I need the information you might find at home. And you are the logical person to find it. I have to be elsewhere, on your business."

"If you are trying to make me feel small, you have," Jean informed him.

Cort nodded and unfolded the papers. "Let me explain all of this to you."

They sat close together, almost touching, while Cort tried to decipher each clause and sentence for Jean. Some of the words were similar to the German she'd studied in school and it seemed his translation of the contract was accurate. But she still had deep, nagging doubts.

Yet she had to make a decision. If she didn't sign, nothing would be done. If the Champagne Rose was really as valuable as Cort said, she would still have the responsibility for it. If Cort was not honest, he would take the jewel through some subterfuge and she would never get anything. To receive something from this deal, she had to take a stance and live with her decision, right or wrong.

"What do you hope to gain?" Jean asked Cort.

"What?"

"Do you want a commission, a percentage?"

"No," Cort said, laughing. "That's not why I'm doing this."

"Then why are you?"

"To help you," Cort told her. "How else will you reach a suitable market for your gem?"

Jean couldn't come up with a cogent response. She stared at the papers before her, then studied Cort's eyes. No matter that the love she had for him was being pushed to its limits by his heavy-handed tactics, she trusted him. She'd seen him in action and had witnessed his caution and competence, his intelligence and resourcefulness.

If anyone could pull this deal together, it was probably Cort.

Jean had just put pen to paper when Pieter entered the library with another man, who wore a brown leather aviator's jacket and carried a sheaf of charts.

"Good, you're still here, Jean," Pieter said. "This is the man who's going to pilot for me tomorrow. I want you to show him the airport nearest your hometown."

Jean blinked and tried to get her bearings. The usually-gloomy Pieter seemed to have a bloom in his cheeks, despite his wounded arm. It was not difficult to point out the airport about twenty miles from her home.

The pilot looked at the mark on the map, then scanned the directory. "We'll have to be out of there by five tomorrow evening," he decided. "This time of year it gets gusty after sundown. That means we'll leave here between noon and one in the afternoon."

"Fine. We'll pick you up at noon, Jean, at your place," Pieter told her breezily. "Now all I have to do is make arrangements for the yacht to be moored in the marina. When the weather is better, I'll hire a crew to deliver it to Hyannis. Now I'm as free as a bird!"

"I didn't say I was going," Jean muttered to herself as she watched Pieter usher the pilot from the room.

"You are, though, aren't you?" Cort asked, taking her hand in his.

Jean could not deny him anything when he

looked at her with such searing eyes.

"All right," she acquiesced. "I'll call Ben, then I'll have to call my father to meet me at the airport."

"So, you finally came back to the old neighborhood." Denise held the door for Jean while her roommate carried her garment bag and duffel bag into the apartment. "Where's your constant companion? Is he suddenly too good to help you?"

Jean shook her head and draped the garment bag over the back of a chair. "He wanted to, but I told him I could manage."

"I'm not so sure I approve of a breach of etiquette like that." Denise closed the door and locked it for the night.

Jean took a deep breath and tossed her purse down on the couch. "I'm slightly put out by him, and I think he sensed it, so when I suggested I could manage, he didn't argue."

"He didn't argue?" Denise repeated. "The man who's been jerking you around for four days decided not to argue with you?"

"We're both a little frazzled," Jean explained. She had been fussing with her bags, as though she was going to carry them off to her room. Then she let go of the handles of the duffel bag and sank onto the couch.

She looked drained, and Denise was upset

with herself that she hadn't seen the fatigue in Jean's eyes before.

"All right, what can I do for you?" Denise asked. "I know. You need a cup of coffee?"

"No," Jean answered with a shake of her head.

"A can of soda?"

"No. Look, I need to get some laundry done. I'm going up home tomorrow to see what I can find out about my great-grandmother."

"He talked you into that?" Denise sat down on the arm of the couch and stared at Jean.

"His cousin is giving me a ride up there in their private jet, no less," Jean told her. "A private jet."

"These people! Are they made of money?"

Jean shrugged. "All I know is that they have that house, a sailboat, and a jet, and they don't seem to have to work."

"Do you suppose Cort is rich?"

"No," she replied, shaking her head. "I think he's a poor cousin. I think he has to work. I guess he just comes here for vacation, maybe mooches off them."

"All the more reason for you to be careful," Denise advised.

"I know," Jean agreed with a sigh. She stood slowly and picked up her bags. "I have to repack and do some handwashing."

"You know that pair of jeans I got that were too heavy to be comfortable? They might be good for up north. You can take them," Denise offered. "What else do you need?"

"Nothing," Jean answered. "I've got a couple of sweaters and a good pair of slacks."

Denise watched as Jean dumped the contents of her duffel bag, sorted laundry, and repacked.

"I don't know about this, Jean," Denise said, planting herself on the end of the bed. "Sure, you're getting a free ride back home, but how will you get back here?"

"I can borrow from Dad and pay him back later," Jean proposed, digging a heavy sweater from the bottom of a bureau drawer. "I haven't asked Dad for anything since I left home, so it's not like I'll be imposing. I'd rather not have to, but what's family for?"

"Jean, I'm afraid it's a wild-goose chase you're going on."

"Then again," Jean mused, putting a sweater into her bag, "it could be the greatest adventure of my life. If I don't do this, I'll never know the truth. I'll always wonder if my great-grandmother stole that brooch from the van Roys. I'll wonder if a van Roy seduced her and . . . and if . . . maybe I'm related to Cort. He seems to think that would be a big problem. I know of second cousins who have married and had perfect children, but he seems to think it would be wrong."

"You're thinking of marrying him?" Denise demanded.

197

"Well, don't you always think about it?" Jean queried. "We get to an age where independence is no longer all it was cracked up to be. The nights get lonely, and you want someone to share your life with on a permanent basis. Sometimes you see someone across a room and you know."

"Is that the way it was?"

Jean gathered a handful of lingerie and headed for the bathroom sink with it. "That's the way it was for me. I saw him across a room and I wanted to touch him. I've never felt that way about anyone before."

Denise lounged against the bathroom door, then hung the bits of lingerie over the shower curtain rod after Jean finished with them. "Do you think Mrs. van Roy washes out a few things every evening?"

Jean laughed. "I don't think she's all that different from you and me. I don't think a lot of money really solves problems. I think it just makes new ones."

"Yeah. Well, I'd like to see, first hand. You know?"

Jean smiled. "Maybe I'll never know, but if I don't take a chance, I haven't even a hope."

"I can't talk you out of going, then?" Denise asked, heading for the kitchen to make a pot of coffee.

"Nope!" Jean called back, following her.

"How much do you think that brooch is

worth?" Denise wondered as they waited for the coffee to go through the machine.

"Cort gave me a figure, but I don't think I should discuss it," Jean hedged.

"Huh! But it's enough to get him all hot and bothered, eh?"

"It's so much that I'd have to spend most of my year's pay to insure it," Jean said, taking mugs from the cupboard and setting them on the counter. "That's why I can't keep it."

"So, if he's on the up-and-up, what would you do with the money?"

Jean glared at Denise. "Why do you keep asking me that? First you tell me I'm stupid to believe in someone who is probably a fraud, then you ask me what I'm going to do with the money!"

For the first time in their friendship Denise backed away. "I'm sorry," she apologized. "It's just that . . . I think of things I'd do if I had a lot of cash. I thought everybody imagined things like that."

"Well, I don't have the slightest idea," Jean countered. "I don't know how much it will be."

"Maybe you're right. See the money first, then decide what to do with it."

That should have been the end of it, but Denise had a hard time sleeping that night. It was more than the coffee that kept her awake. She was genuinely concerned about Jean and didn't want to see her swindled or, worse, brokenhearted.

But something had happened. Jean usually took her advice. For some reason she wasn't this time.

Maybe Jean had to keep her own counsel about Cort van Roy and the brooch and the trip back to Pennsylvania. Yes, sometimes a person had to do what was right even if it wasn't smart.

Still, Denise couldn't help worrying.

Jean removed her bottle of hand lotion and the paperback book by Tolstoy from her locker. To Jean it seemed like a very final act, even though she had convinced Ben Evans not to replace her for at least two weeks.

Ben forced his lips together in a disapproving line. "Do you really know what you're doing, Jean?" he asked, being paternal for the first time since she had known him.

"Look, the worst that can happen is that I'll spend some time with my father," Jean assured him as she dropped the bottle and the book into her purse. "I haven't seen him in two years. The weather will be awful, but it won't be the first time I've seen snow."

"But what about this Dutch fellow?" Ben asked. "I really don't like the sound of this."

"I'll be all right." Jean gave Ben's rounded shoulder half a hug. "Maybe it's time I was moving on, anyway. You've got to admit I've done everything here there is to do."

"Don't be afraid to come back," he said as she started toward the time clock to punch out.

"Love ya', Ben," she called back over her shoulder with a little more bravado than she was feeling.

Cort was waiting for her in the parking lot, his face grim. She noticed the lump under his jacket where it covered his holster. They went to the bank where she removed the Champagne Rose from the safety-deposit box. Jean inspected it in the strong clear light of the vault before handing it to him.

"One last chance to back out," Cort offered, his hand poised over the brooch.

She studied his eyes. The one that had been bruised looked almost normal now. Seeing them in this light, more equal and unflinching, she could do nothing but trust him.

She knew that she had never really trusted a man before. She had always been able to walk away without regrets. Even though she had not given Cort the fullest extent of her love, she trusted him and therefore was vulnerable.

"What is the van Roy Champagne Rose to me?" she asked. "It's not for me to own. It would be best for someone who can take proper care of it to own it. This wild ride I've been on for the past few days has to end."

His hand closed over the Champagne Rose.

After holding it to the light for a moment, he dropped the gem into a cloth pouch and tucked it into his inside pocket.

Jean didn't want the empty feeling she had inside. It made the return to her apartment to pick up her duffel bag a chore.

The place over the deli seemed so empty and silent. She wished Denise had been there, but they had said their goodbyes that morning. She didn't want their parting to be so final. She knew that whatever she learned back home in Pennsylvania was going to change her life forever.

When they reached the private airfield, Cort drove to the hangar where the jet was readied for takeoff.

The plane was smaller than Jean had expected, but it was sleek and polished. Jean wondered if there was any way she could gracefully refuse to go up in it. But everyone around her seemed so eager about the trip that she could not bring herself to voice any misgivings.

Besides, flying this way was a privilege, an experience to file away for the dreary days life often dealt.

Taking her duffel bag, Cort helped Jean into the waiting jet.

"Remember what I said about the boat?" Jean asked him, looking around the well-appointed but cramped cabin.

"Yes," he said, his eyes questioning.

"It goes double for planes." Her tone did not come out quite as kidding as she wanted it, and she knew that Cort sensed her apprehension.

"Don't be afraid," Cort soothed, his hands resting comfortingly on her shoulders.

"I used to be frightened myself," Kiki confessed, following them into the cabin. "But you get used to it."

Jean sat down in the passenger seat directly behind the pilot's position and looked up at Cort. Kiki arranged the armload of belongings she thought were essential to making her trip bearable. Cort leaned over the pilot's seat and clasped Jean's hand.

"Oh, I forgot something," Kiki mumbled and exited the plane again.

Cort turned his head to watch Kiki leave. Jean tried to memorize each detail of his broad forehead and neatly-trimmed dark hair.

"Do you have my father's telephone number?"

He chuckled. "In three places. I'm used to doing things in triplicate."

"Why won't you give me yours?" Jean asked. It was one of the few points she had lost in their settling of matters the night before.

"I've got so many little trips to make to take care of the Rose, darling," he explained, moving to appropriate the seat Kiki would be occupying on the flight. "All you'd get is my answering machine, and I'd have to call you anyway."

Why did his sensible answer discourage her

so? Again Jean felt empty inside, afraid that this was the last time she would see Cort. She had willfully become one of the biggest fools in the history of the world, to fall in love with this man and let him take not only the Rose, but her heart as well.

He wrapped his arms around her and held her to his solid chest for a long moment. When she looked up at his gray-gold eyes, she saw him smiling, but somehow that smile was not reassuring.

"Why are you trembling so?" Cort asked softly.

"I don't know."

"You can't be frightened." He laughed gently.

"I think I could be."

"Oh, no, not you! Not the woman who sprang to Pieter's aid the other night, who bound his wound and calmed Kiki with a look."

"That was nothing, next to this."

"This is nothing, my dear, next to that." Cort sighed. "Where is the adventurer, the risk taker?"

"She should have found a safer place to be by now."

"She is in my arms, and I wish we were not parting. It won't be for long."

His lips settled on hers for one last rapturous moment. She closed her eyes, wanting the world to end now, before he left her, before she embarked on a fool's errand.

But the plane was being jostled by the footfalls of Kiki and the pilot boarding, and Cort let her go—much too soon.

Cort didn't really say goodbye. He merely got up and moved aside so that Kiki could get to her seat.

Kiki was holding a mohair wrap and the soft leather coat she had worn the night Pieter had been shot. For a moment she seemed to be considering them, then she dropped the coat into Jean's lap.

"This will be great for all the running around you have to do when you get home," she said. "You'll find that leather blocks the wind very well."

"I couldn't . . ." Jean protested, even as her fingers reveled in the buttery texture of the leather.

"I told you you can mail it to me when you don't need it anymore," Kiki said, fastening her seat belt. "Once we get to ten thousand feet or so, you'll probably want to wrap it around yourself. Did you bring anything to read?"

Jean reached into her purse and pulled out Tolstoy. Kiki made a face and handed her a sensational best-seller.

"Now, this will keep your mind occupied!" she promised with a wry smile.

The pilot was putting on a bulky set of earphones and adjusting his seat. Cort had left the plane momentarily and was now helping Pieter to the co-pilot seat, protecting Pieter's injured arm from being jostled.

"Have a good trip, everyone," Cort said at last, with one long last look at Jean, then slammed the cabin door.

The pilot waited for Cort to be clear of the plane before he signaled a waiting crewman to start a power unit, a cart-mounted generator to start the turbojet engines.

Jean watched Cort return to his car by the hangar. He got into the vehicle slowly, as though lingering as long as he could. As soon as the pilot began to taxi the plane, Cort closed the door of his car and was driving toward the exit by the time the plane was airborne.

Kiki patted Jean's arm with her manicured fingers. "Don't worry," she yelled over the noise of the engines and the air swooshing under the wings.

Kiki's face was so serene that Jean wondered what Cort's cousin knew that she didn't.

Cort stopped by the agency where José had dropped off the car Pieter had rented for their winter vacation. It was a relief to let José drive him back to the mansion.

Never had Cort felt so alone, and he had spent most of his life alone. He had gone to the same American prep school Pieter had been sent to. Having a cousin who was also a classmate had been the biggest joy in his young life. But this emptiness was worse than what he had experienced in those days following his graduation. After a dinner with Pieter and his parents, Cort had boarded a night flight to the Middle Eastern country where his father was posted.

Yes, it was worse to know what he must do took priority over the love he had found so unexpectedly.

José, having been in Cort's employ for four years, knew not to interrupt his dark moods. They would soon be back in more familiar territory, where they would go about their business, sure of themselves.

Damn! Being in love was as strange as being on the moon, the last accessible place it seemed that Cort hadn't been. One moment, holding Jean in his arms, could be more than the heaven he had dreamed of. To be so very far apart was a hell worse than the Italian prison where he had posed as a convict to trick a man into revealing where a fortune in jewels had been buried.

The car was a small coupe, likewise rented, and would be picked up later that afternoon. As Cort was getting out, José was already going through it to be certain they left nothing of their own behind. Cort paused and watched him, almost hoping that he'd find something Jean had left behind, a handkerchief or an earring. But he knew he was clutching at straws.

He touched the pouch that held the Champagne Rose, then turned toward the house.

Mrs. Ghent looked up defiantly when Cort entered the kitchen. She was packing up the perishable foods to take somewhere—home with her, he supposed.

"So, they got off?" she asked, her gnarled hand resting on a jar she had just placed in an open cardboard box.

"Yes," he replied with a disconsolate nod.

"You like the young lady—Jean—huh?" Mrs. Ghent wheedled, a hard edge to her voice.

He nodded.

"Sad. Well, I'll go as soon as I finish here," Mrs. Ghent told him, moving to a cupboard that stood open. "I've left you and your man some sandwiches in the refrigerator."

The last thing he wanted to think about was food, but he thanked her. "Mrs. Ghent, do you have a few moments that we could talk?"

"Sorry, no," she grumbled, not revealing the source of the deep-seated anger that was obviously consuming her.

"I just want to ask you about when you first worked here. Do you remember anything unusual happening with any of the servants, or the young people in the family?"

"I'm an old woman," Mrs. Ghent explained. "I don't have time to remember all the shenanigans that went on here in the early days. My father always told me it was best for servants to forget the peccadilloes and shortcomings of their families. That way, you kept your job."

"Can you tell me anything about a family named Mc—Mc—" In pausing to check his memory of the name Jean had mentioned, Cort lost any hope of getting a response from Mrs. Ghent.

"Look, you've always been nice to work for. But I'm not pleased with the sound of things when Mr. Pieter and Miss Kiki argue over whether they are ever going to come back here again. After all these years of saving them these months every year! I could have been working for someone else, you know! As it is, I have to do catering, and it's a sometime thing. I'd rather be working all the time for one family, kind of steady, than like this. But I'm an old woman, Mr. van Roy, and who's going to hire me?"

"I understand," Cort apologized, and backed toward the door. "I'm sorry."

He went to his room and changed into more casual clothing. He didn't like to travel in a suit. His leather jacket was better at concealing the pistol he would have to wear every moment until the van Roy Champagne Rose was safely locked away in a vault in Antwerp.

José tapped at his door, then came in to pack his bags. "Is there anything more to do?" he asked, glancing around the room.

"No," Cort answered, lifting his jacket from the back of a chair. He put the pouch holding the Champagne Rose into an inside pocket and zipped it closed.

"Your formal suit!" José exclaimed, pushing things around in the closet. "I took it to the cleaners and forgot it's not supposed to be ready until tomorrow."

"Damn!" Cort swore. "I'll have to ask Mrs. Ghent to pick it up and send it to me."

"She already left," José said.

"Where's the receipt?" Cort asked. "I'll call the cleaners and tell them if I don't come back for it in a month to send it to Paris."

But, I'll be back, he vowed.

As the plane swooped down from the late-afternoon sky, causing the tops of the pines that guarded the airport to bend, Jean cinched the leather coat about her. The last rays of the winter sun sent long shadows across drifts of snow. She shivered just looking at the mounds of white.

The pilot landed the plane smoothly. Jean wished that she could have been as calm about this whole flight. They taxied close to the tiny terminal, and all filed out to stretch their legs.

Kiki tugged the full hood of her mohair wrap up over her head, then hunched her shoulders against the wind.

"Are you sure someone will be here to meet you?" she asked Jean as they hurried toward the building behind the pilot and Pieter.

"Dad said he would be," Jean told her, feeling the sting of cold air on her cheeks. A frigid blast seemed to reach into her soul and increased the uncertainty she felt about this whole escapade.

Then she spotted her father with his nose pressed almost against the glass. His eyes were bright, and a smile slowly lighted his whole face.

In an instant she had entered the warmth of the building and of his embrace.

"My gal is coming up in the world." He chuckled as he patted her shoulder. "Such a plane! Such a way to travel!"

"These people were kind enough to give me a ride, Dad," Jean said, and introduced Kiki and Pieter. Pieter drifted away after a brief handshake. Kiki stood close by, stomped snow from her leather boots and blew on her hands.

"Can I have just a minute with you?" Kiki asked Jean. "I know you and your father probably want to get going."

"I'll take your bag to the car," her father told Jean.

"Yes?" Jean asked, turning to Kiki.

"You might not realize it since Cort is so close about his feelings. But I think he's in love with you. I've never seen him as interested in a woman. Things are going to work out, Jean. Just let him come to you."

"That's my only option," Jean told her.

Kiki leaned close and lowered her voice. "We'll be cousins," she whispered, winking.

"Thank you for everything. I hope Pieter's arm heals quickly."

"So do I. Go! Don't keep your father waiting."

Jean hurried out to the parking lot and got into the unfamiliar car her father was warming up.

"New car, Dad?" she asked, trying to control her chattering teeth.

"Yep! The old one needed a new transmission, so I traded it in," he explained, backing out of the space. "It's good to have you home, but it's a bit of a surprise, isn't it? Why come home when you have all that sun and warmth in Florida?"

"It's a long story," Jean said with a sigh, clutching her coat around her.

"Now's the time to tell me," her father said.

He listened attentively as she told him the story from beginning to end, leaving out only the details that would have told him of her attraction to Cort. She wasn't ready to share that with her father just yet.

"I need to know anything you can tell me about my great-grandmother and the jewelry that was passed down to Mom," Jean summed it all up.

Tom Barbour shook his white head and

212

shrugged his shoulders under his dark herring-bone overcoat. "I've never felt it my place to listen to the gossip in your mother's family," he told her. "It wasn't my business."

"I was afraid you'd say that." Jean exhaled and watched the white puff of her breath expand in the space between her and the windshield.

"You might go to the newspaper and check the morgue files on the Baker and Finney families," he suggested. "It might be a little harder to get to the cemetery records and the county records. And I have no idea if they had a family Bible or who would have it, but we'll check on it. Maybe make a few phone calls tonight."

"Yes, I guess that's the best way to start," Jean agreed. "But it all seems pretty morbid."

"Well, that's all there is to do," he said. "But first we'll get a good dinner in you. Shirley's fixing pot roast."

Jean settled into the seat and tried to feel some warmth from the car heater. At least her father was happy. His face lit up every time he mentioned Shirley.

At first when her father remarried, Jean had had a hard time adjusting to someone taking her mother's place in his life. She had left town rather than watch what was happening. She'd said it was because she had come to an impasse with her boyfriend, and there were no interesting jobs around.

She had put the best face on it. She had wanted to give her father and his new wife space to establish their relationship without having to deal with her, too. The truth was that she had been hurt. But now the years had dulled the aching, and she was glad to see that her father was happy.

The conclusion that she had reached the end of her relationship with her boyfriend struck her as ironic now.

Bob had announced that he wanted to join the local police force and entered an independent academy to try this vocation. Jean had recoiled from the thought, even though Bob had compiled impressive statistics to prove being a police officer in a small town placed him in very little danger.

Now her life was totally entangled with a man who lived in more danger than Bob could ever think of getting into! How very strange life sometimes became.

It was about time she went home and settled some long-standing issues. Maybe the mystery of the van Roy Champagne Rose was the least of them.

Cort shed his overcoat in Heinrich Plautt's office, glad to be in out of the damp cold of Antwerp's winter, to place the van Roy Champagne Rose in Heinrich's state-of-the-art vault.

Plautt was a tall, sophisticated man, always neatly attired and businesslike. There was a warm smile on his face as he took his seat at his desk.

"So," Plautt asked with a touch of anticipation in his voice, "what are you bringing me? What is all the excitement about?"

"Give me a moment to collect myself," Cort pleaded, taking a deep breath as he sank into a chair across from the gem dealer. "I've been traveling since last night with this item in my possession. I'm tired of watching over my shoulder every step of the way."

"Have you been followed?" Heinrich asked, alarmed.

"Only by the demons of paranoia and lack of sleep, in all probability." Cort laughed and reached into his jacket pocket.

His pistol still weighed heavily against his ribs. But the lighter weight of the small pouch had been like a burning coal since noon the day before. He couldn't decide if he was pleased to be rid of the burden or not.

"This," he said, loosening the string on the pouch and shaking the brooch into his palm.

Heinrich gasped and reached for his jeweler's loupe. "Even from this distance, it appears to be magnificent!"

Cort felt the weight of the brooch in his hand for a treasured moment, then extended it to Heinrich for his eager appraisal.

"Ah, my old friend, where have you found such a beauty?" Heinrich wanted to know, adjusting his eye to the loupe. He gasped in awe as he rotated the gem slowly with his manicured fingertips.

"It had been in my family for many years, first as an uncut stone, then cut and mounted as it is," Cort explained. He leaned back to recount the story slowly.

"In the last century, one of my relatives in the Transvaal was out riding, and her horse threw her. When she was found, the rough stone was in her hand. Investigation led her father to a great pipe of diamonds, which made a great deal of the van Roy family's fortune. This particular stone was smuggled back to the Netherlands. Years later my great-grandfather had it cut and set for his wife. The family legend says that it was stolen in 1925. But it turned up again last Saturday night, worn by a lovely young lady. She thought it was a piece of glass because her grandmother used to give it to her to play with."

"Hm!" Heinrich breathed. "And you want it sold at our auction next week."

"No," Cort said tightly. "I want to keep it. I have a plan."

Heinrich raised one eyebrow and nodded for Cort to continue.

"As you know, I own an extensive collection of art," Cort said. "I don't have a copy of my

216

inventory with me, but I can provide you with one easily enough. I would put up sufficient pieces to cover the highest bid anyone might come up with."

Heinrich tapped his fingers on the edge of his desk. "You want this gem very much, don't you? Yes, something could very probably be worked out. As always, it is good to do business with you."

Chapter Ten

When Cort had secured a ticket for the Paris train and settled into a window seat, he leaned back and stared into the night. The lights of Antwerp soon gave way to the clusters of houses in villages and then to scattered farms and forests. Cort let his tired mind review what he had accomplished.

The Champagne Rose was safe, but there was the risk of it soon being out of his possession. He faced the formidable challenge of raising the money to outbid anyone else who might want to buy it.

He had never thought of himself as a wealthy man. Surely others in his own family, and in the larger, extended van Roy family, possessed much more than he did. But he'd put his knowledge of art to good use over the years. He had assembled a small collection of canvases and sculptures that was admired by some and envied by others.

But was the Champagne Rose reason enough to sacrifice it all? There was one factor that was worth the sacrifice of all he owned: Jean.

He envisioned her face beyond the darkened glass of the railroad car window. Her strength in the face of disaster held him in awe. Her humor was endearing. Her smile breathtaking.

Cort imagined Jean again as he had first seen her, wearing the Champagne Rose on the front of the midnight-blue gown. He remembered the physical reaction he'd had at first glance. Discounting that the same picture included the image of the thief DePesca, his heart raced anew. Had some dowager affixed the Rose to the bodice of a similar dress, he would probably have felt a kick of recognition, but not the overwhelming involvement that overtook him.

He knew, when he hustled Jean from the ballroom, that from that moment on he was including her in his life. There was no discussion about that.

But the way she had proven herself in tending to Pieter's wound had cemented their fates. He could have walked away before that moment, nursed his own wounded heart, and lived to love another time. But Jean had proved to be made of the stern stuff he required of a wife. Whoever married him was going to need a backbone of steel. Such a woman was Jean.

And he loved her.

* * *

The last of the embers glowed, and an occasional flame flickered on the hearth. Jean didn't want to leave the living room, although she had long ago said good night to her father and his wife. She sat holding an empty coffee mug, listening to the wind howl beyond the stout walls of the house she had grown up in.

She knew her bedroom would be cold. There was nothing in her small bag to warm her in that narrow bed. Why had she come home? Why had she allowed Cort to talk her into this insanity?

So far, she had spent hours at the local newspaper's office tracking her ancestors' comings and goings, births, marriages, and deaths. When she had jotted down everything she could find, she had shaken her head and pronounced it hopeless.

The telephone rang, and Jean hurried across the room to answer it before it roused her father.

"Barbours'," she said, knowing that whoever was at the other end would be expecting someone else to answer.

"Jean?" Cort's voice came to her. "Good, you got home all right."

"Yes," Jean answered, suddenly feeling a thrill of warmth go through her. "And you?"

"I'm just back in Paris. The sun is coming up."

"You're at home?"

"Yes, finally. And the Rose is safely in a vault in Antwerp, waiting for the auction next Tuesday evening."

"Ah, that's a relief."

"And how are you?"

"Cold. But my father and his wife are trying to make me comfortable. Today I went to the newspaper and tried to trace my family. It wasn't very fruitful."

"Stay with it, Jean," he encouraged her.

"Of course," she agreed. It was easy for him to say; his work was over.

"I gave the auctioneer a figure we would not go below," he told her. "You will have money to do whatever you want when this is over."

"Yes, I will, won't I?"

"I must go now, Jean. I haven't slept since Wednesday morning."

"Sweet dreams, then." When she hung up, Shirley was standing in the doorway.

"I thought I heard the phone ring," Shirley said, cinching her robe around her.

"My friend in Paris . . ." Jean started to explain.

"Is everything all right?"

"He just wanted me to know that the Champagne Rose got to Belgium safely."

"Oh. Well, I guess you can rest more easily now." Shirley seemed to notice Jean's dubious expression. "Maybe you need something more to

221

help you sleep."

"I'm not used to the cold." Jean sighed, crossing her arms in front of her.

"I'll find you more blankets," Shirley offered and scurried off.

Jean left her empty mug in the kitchen and went to her bedroom. Shirley was spreading another cover over the chenille spread that was already there.

"This quilt will go over the whole bed," Shirley pointed out, trying to keep her voice just above a whisper. "It's been in the family for years. My aunt—You know, Jean, I think I do remember someone who knew your grandmother, maybe even your great-grandmother. I'll see if I can get permission for you to go see her in the nursing home."

"I'd appreciate that." Jean stifled a yawn, willing to grasp at one last straw.

"Well, you should get a good night's sleep now, dear." Shirley gave the quilt a last loving pat and left the room.

There was a faint scent of cedar on the blankets which lulled Jean into a feeling of warmth and security, undisturbed by the howling of the chill wind outside or the uneasy thoughts of Cort. She slept for what seemed like the first time in a week.

In her dreams she felt Cort's presence, as though they were sharing the bed, its comfort, and its warmth. In a wordless, unhurried communion they held each other in a passion that had no boundaries, no rules.

When morning came, Jean wanted to clutch the remnants of her dream around her to sustain her through the gray dawn. But somewhere between the warmth of the covers and the cold tile floor of the bathroom, the fantasy evaporated.

The old lady in the nursing home was a dear. As her blue-veined hands traced the patterns in the afghan draped over her lap, she rocked to some inner rhythm and thought back over the decades of her life.

Jean read the names from the list she had formed at the newspaper and waited patiently for the woman to recall each one.

"Could Great-grandma's first child have been, well, could it have been . . ." Jean approached the thought obliquely. She was as afraid of dashing all her own hopes as she was of offending this woman, who had been so forthcoming.

"Could she have had a bun in the oven when she came back from Florida?" the woman asked, her eyes suddenly sparkling. "No, darlin'. Could never have happened, not with Tom Finney. He was too hidebound to have accepted another man's child, or to have, well, you know . . . Men who make mistakes in their lives tend to be more tolerant of others' frailties than Tom ever was."

Jean frowned. She was as far from the truth about the Champagne Rose as she had been in Palm Beach.

"There was a lot of gossip around that spring, but I don't recall a breath of it having to do with your great-gramma." The old woman frowned as though she were trying to sort through her memories for something important. But at the end, she shook her head.

"I'd better go," Jean said at last, rising from her chair. "I don't want to tire you. Maybe I'll come again before I go back to Florida."

Driving through town, Jean stopped at the drugstore to get something for her throat, which was becoming sore. She was paying for her purchase when the glass door of the store opened and a man in a police officer's uniform came in.

"Ha!" Bob Coleman laughed. "I wondered when we'd run into each other, Jean. Heard you were in town. Saw you park your dad's car down the street."

"So you followed me," Jean accused, dropping the bag with her cough drops into her purse.

"Can't help my police training," he defended. "Why are you in town?"

"Personal business," Jean told him, pushing past him to get out to the street.

"Look, I want to talk to you," Bob explained. "Come over to the station. My break is up and

I've got to check in."

"I'll walk over with you," Jean offered, "but I've got things to do."

"Sure. Come on, humor an old boyfriend," Bob urged, digging his hands into the pockets of his navy nylon parka.

Jean looked up at him skeptically. Her sun had once risen and set on him. But she had begun to doubt her commitment to him when Bob had told her he wanted to become an officer of the law.

"What do you want to know?" she asked.

"What kind of trouble are you in?"

"None that I know of."

"I was working the desk when Palm Beach PD requested a background check on you," Bob revealed, his voice full of astonishment. "Then Interpol sent a request the next day. Interpol! You know how it is in a small town. Everyone knows everyone else's business. Everybody was looking at me and wondering if I knew something—"

"That's stupid. We broke up years ago. Are you married?"

"No. Are you?"

"No."

They had to wait for the light to change before stepping off the curb and crossing the street.

"Whatever you've been doing, it looks like you're not doing too bad," Bob appraised, motioning toward the leather coat Jean wore.

"It's borrowed from a friend."

"Sure." Bob chuckled, looking away.

"Interpol doesn't chase stolen coats," Jean informed him, trying to follow his mental processes.

"The trouble with being a policeman, Jeanie," Bob explained, taking her arm as the light changed, "is that you start thinking like a criminal. The man who has an affinity for the criminal mind is the one who goes far in this field."

"Now you tell me," she said in mock derision.

He nodded. "The facts are that we've had two requests for background checks on you. We responded by telling the agencies that you are, as far as we know, above reproach. Then you show up here. You've got to admit it seems a little strange." He lowered his voice. "Are you running? Do you need protection? Or have you stooped to a life of crime?"

"You'd probably get a big laugh out of what happened to me," Jean told him. "And I'd tell you, except I don't know the whole story myself."

"Try me."

"No. I'm shivering here. I think I'm coming down with a cold. Last Sunday I was cruising on the Atlantic on a sailboat. Now I'm freezing in this awful snow." Jean squinted up into the leaden sky and hunched her shoulders.

"Come inside. We'll talk. It's a slow day.

Maybe the chief can help."

She looked up at his face and saw that he was not going to let her go easily. "Darn. All right! Just to satisfy you and whoever else thinks it might be fun to find out why Interpol wants to know what I've been up to."

She waited for him to open the door for her because her hands were clenched in tight fists for warmth.

Bob introduced her to the chief and a lieutenant. They sat around a table, drinking coffee from foam cups and listening to her story. Occasionally they asked questions when they thought it necessary.

"You say you gave this Interpol man your gem to take back to Europe to sell?" the chief asked.

"He called last night to say it was safe in Antwerp and he was back in Paris," Jean informed him.

"And you trust him?"

Jean knew she should have been able to say it firmly, without equivocation, that she had infinite faith in Cort. But she hesitated.

"If the gem had really meant anything to me, I would not have," she said at last. "Or maybe I'm telling myself it doesn't mean much to me. Anyway, I'm trying to find out why my great-grandmother had the van Roy Champagne Rose in the first place. I thought I might find the answer back here. But so far, my great-grandmother appears to be the fine lady I was led to believe all along."

"You say she worked for the McClellan family?" the chief asked, pouring himself more coffee. "Humph! I can't say that that rings any bells."

"I thought," Jean explained, "as a last resort, I'd go back to the newspaper and check their morgue file. It's my last link."

Bob was sorting through the papers in his hand, the requests that had come for the background checks on Jean. "There's nothing here about the man who's at the bottom of all this, Jean. Let me check on him."

She wrote the name on the scratch pad in front of her and pushed it across the table to Bob.

"Are you staying with your father?" Bob asked. When she nodded, he continued. "I'll get in touch with you there when we hear anything."

Cort strode into Robert's office and dropped a sheaf of papers on his superior's desk.

"Again," he declared, as though they were in the middle of a discussion, "I want to get out of this position, Robert. It's standing between me and a normal life. I want to live without suspecting every shadow and fearing for the life of everyone I speak to."

Robert looked up from his desk with eyes that were bored and tired from the paperwork he constantly shuffled.

"You are too good an investigator for us to lose you at this point," he argued, as he had said so many times before. "You have the devious mind of a criminal, the instinct to know what a man will do next. I cannot let you go."

"But I must—"

"The blonde." Robert sighed, looking away. Why is it always a blonde?"

"I have never been sidetracked before," Cort defended.

"Perhaps not you. But it is always a blonde. Even for me it was a blonde."

Cort was about to turn and leave the office when Robert sighed again and shifted in his chair.

"Perhaps you are too valuable to be out in the field," Robert posed. "We need knowledgeable operatives so desperately that perhaps we should use you to train other men. I'll see if we can work that out with my bosses. But don't think you can just walk away from us.

He got up from his desk and reached for the jacket he had hung over the back of his chair. "Come with me," he ordered.

Robert led the way to the office of the chief of the bureau and sketched out the proposal with an economy of words that left questions in the chief's mind.

"Compromised?" the chief demanded, clutching at the word. "How are you compromised, sir?" he questioned, glaring at Cort.

The chief always turned very formal when he faced Cort, in deference to his family's background. Robert had long since ceased to be impressed.

"I would have second thoughts at placing myself in danger," Cort explained. "This last operation involved a part of my own family, and a woman I have become, well . . ."

"I see. And you feel you would be better utilized in an instructional post and in possibly planning operations."

"That was my suggestion," Robert interceded. "Cort proposed to leave us altogether."

"I'm sorry, we can't have that. The other, yes. Yes!" he agreed enthusiastically. "And I understand the recent operation took up your holiday time."

"Yes, sir," Cort told him. "It also left me with some personal business to attend to, both here in Europe and back in the States."

The chief turned to his assistant, who had been hovering near a computer terminal during the discussion. "Yves? It's a good idea. A solution to the problem we were discussing last month. Remove this man's name from the list of active investigators and transfer it to Operations. You understand that it will take a week or so for us to make the necessary adjustments, don't you, sir? Until then, you are relieved of duty to handle your personal business and prepare for your new duties."

"Thank you, sir," Cort said, slightly bewildered but pleased nonetheless.

"This doesn't mean that you're free of the dangers you've been living with," Robert explained as they left the chief's office. "Cort, you know too much. You're too hated by the criminals of this world to be less than vigilant."

"I understand," Cort agreed. "But in time we are all forgotten."

"One hopes!" Robert exclaimed, slapping him on the shoulder.

Cort left the bureau office and went to visit his mother and father in the Dutch embassy. The Princess Erricha met him with a long embrace and a kiss on each cheek.

"Did you enjoy your holiday in America?" she asked.

"No, Mama, but I met the woman I want for my wife," Cort replied.

His father laughed, a deep sound that comforted Cort more than the safety of the Rose or his return to Paris had. "Now you know how I felt when I met your lovely mother," the duke said. "The joy of the love, the fear of what was to come."

"Jean is the current owner of the van Roy Rose," he told his father. "She allowed me to take it to Antwerp to be auctioned. I must have

231

it, if I have to sell my Mondrian and all my post-Impressionists!"

Princess Erricha lowered her straight body to a damask chair and looked at him with interest. "My darling, you must want the Rose very much."

They had a long conversation over dinner that raised Cort's spirits about the prospects of regaining the Rose. Yet he was still in some anguish at being separated from Jean. When he returned to his home in a fashionable suburb, the telephone was ringing.

As he took his key from the lock, he hoped he would reach the phone in time and that it would be Jean.

"I knew if I held on long enough you'd answer," Pieter's voice responded to his greeting.

Of course it would not be Jean. He hadn't given her this number.

"Pieter! How is everything? How's your arm?" he asked his cousin.

"The arm's coming along fine," Pieter answered. "And I think coming home was the right thing. Kiki is much happier, and Willie was overjoyed to see us. We're going to Stowe this weekend, and I'm going to spend the day on the bunny slope with him. I want to talk to you about something."

"What?" Cort asked, dropping his overcoat over the back of a chair.

"We've about decided to sell the place in Palm

Beach," Pieter informed him. "We're going to spend more time up here with Willie. I thought we'd give you first refusal on it before we put it on the market."

Cort took a deep breath. "I wish I could say I'd take it, but I can't see how I can make an offer right now."

"Well, I don't expect we'll unload it with a snap of our fingers. I'll give you three months to decide, let's say, before I list it anywhere."

"I appreciate that, but I'll know much sooner than that if I'll have the reason to take it off your hands. By the way," Cort said slowly, formulating his plan as he went, "may I have the use of the place late next week, probably for the weekend?"

"Sure. Call Mrs. Ghent the day or so before you want to arrive and she'll do whatever has to be done to open the house. Do you have her number?"

Cort scribbled it on the last page of his pocket address book, then chatted for a few more minutes with Pieter before hanging up.

He had turned on only one lamp when he had answered the phone. Now he turned on two more lamps in the parlor and sprawled thoughtfully on a couch. Damn! He'd missed a step in his plan.

Cort retrieved his briefcase from the place he usually dropped it by the door. Impatiently he shuffled through the contents until he found

233

the painstakingly accurate sketch he'd made on his way to Antwerp. He could probably reach Albert at this time of night.

Albert, the best paste artist in France. Yes, things could come together!

He heard a noise in the apartment and realized that José was there, probably in the kitchen. When he had hung up the phone after speaking to Albert, he saw José waiting in the doorway that led to the dining room.

"Can I do something for you, sir?"

"Ah! There's a lot to do, and I don't know where to start," Cort told him, invigorated.

"Perhaps with something to eat—"

"Coffee! Lots of coffee. I'm selling the painting in the study."

"The Mondrian?" José gasped, as though the thought horrified him.

"I'll put something else there," he mused. "Perhaps the street scene I bought last summer."

"But, sir . . ." José studied him, then shrugged.

A few minutes later when the paintings had been shifted around, Cort studied the room and smiled.

"Why didn't I think of that before?" he wondered, pleased with himself.

José shrugged and brushed a bit of dust from the frame of the picture he held. Cort never guessed at his servant's thoughts. But José would approve if he knew why his employer was acting so strangely. He probably already suspected.

Jean had spread all her notes on the kitchen table and was going through them once more. Her father poured himself a mug of coffee and lowered himself into his usual chair.

"So?" he asked.

"Nothing!" Jean exclaimed in quiet exasperation. "I thought when I went back and looked up the McClellan family that I'd find the key to all of this, but it wasn't there, either."

"Perhaps no news is good news," he suggested.

"I hardly think that's what Cort expects, or wants, to hear."

"It doesn't matter what he wants or expects," her father reminded her. "All you have to offer him is the truth as you have found it. He will have to be satisfied."

Jean sighed and rested her face in her hands. "Perhaps the awful doubts I have about Cort are the reality," she confessed. "Perhaps he is a con man who sent me on this wild-goose chase to keep me occupied while he does some chicanery."

Her father's face appeared more lined than usual in the light from the lamp over the table. "Is that what concerns you most? That he has duped you out of the Rose?"

"Hardly! I've convinced myself that the Rose means nothing to me."

"Is it real?"

Jean laughed. "What would all this be about if it were a fake? No, Dad, the brooch has to be real. There are pictures of it in family albums."

"Then what of the man?"

"Aha! The crux of the problem. The man."

Her father cradled his coffee mug in both hands and studied his daughter for a long moment. "You're in love with him," he stated.

Jean paused for a long moment. "Yes."

"And that frightens you."

"Where could it go from here, Dad? We are literally from two different worlds. I've learned to be independent, to pull my own weight, to support myself. I'd die without a purpose in my life, and I saw how empty his cousin's wife's life is. I couldn't live that way. And to go to Europe to live—so far away from you? Even in Florida, I knew I could get on a plane and be here in three hours if you needed me, but—"

"Airlines fly there, too," he reminded her. "Besides, I have Shirley."

"Yes," Jean said thoughtfully. "You're very happy, aren't you?"

"We are," he said softly.

"I was thinking of you, singularly."

"I'm very happy," he assured her. "It's different, very different from what I had with your

236

mother. We loved each other, but it was so serious. We had to struggle to have a home, to make a living and raise you, to put you through college. But it's different with Shirley. We're companions first, and that gives us a freedom your mother and I didn't have."

Jean frowned at him. "Even when it's right, are there ever any doubts?"

"Yes. There are always doubts, at first. I don't expect you to understand, darling, because you're still too young. Sometime maybe you will, but it's not important now. Jean, if you love this man, and he is honest, and loves you, then don't be afraid to take that step. Certainly don't hold back for anything that is here in Pennsylvania. Don't be tied to what you think I need from you. I have Shirley. Maybe, when I retire in a few years, we'll decide there is nothing to hold us here, either. Besides, I could visit Europe. It might be fun."

"I can't do anything more . . ." Jean mused, glancing down at the papers in front of her.

The telephone rang, and she answered it at the kitchen counter.

"Good, Jean, you're still there," Bob's voice came to her, breathless and reluctant. "Look, I've got news, of a sort."

"What is it?"

"First of all, Jeanie, we're not awfully used to sending requests for information to foreign agencies," he said, exasperation in his voice.

"I've stuck this out, doing it on my own time, because it was really not our department's business. I've sent three requests. Interpol says that they don't currently have an investigator named Cort van Roy. Chief says I might ask them if they had an agent by that name in the past, but I don't hold out much hope."

"You're kidding." Jean felt as though she was going to fall through the floor.

"Like I said, Jeanie, I wasn't satisfied the first time, so I tried it three times. According to them, he doesn't seem to exist."

"I don't understand."

"Neither do I," Bob told her. "I believed your story; I still do. I'm so sorry."

"Well, thank you for your trouble," Jean said, leaning against the counter for support.

"What are friends for? What are you going to do now?"

"I don't know. Go back to Florida, I guess."

"Goodbye, Jeanie." It was the finality in his tone that made the tears start.

Jean could not get a seat on a flight to Florida until Friday of the next week. When she called to tell Denise that she was coming back, her roommate was glad to hear from her. But Denise voiced hopes that Jean would have called to say she was going directly to Paris and wanted her belongings sent there. Jean nodded in sad agreement.

In the empty days that stood between her and

her departure, Jean bundled into warm clothing and walked the familiar streets of her hometown. She was discouraged as much with its disarray as with her own heartbreak.

Over the years that she had been growing up, the refineries had been closed as the oil fields had gone dry. The steel mills had lost contracts to larger mills in bigger cities or in foreign countries. A decade before the interstate highway system had bypassed the once bustling valley. Now factories were silent and stores closed. Homes were for sale on every block. People were leaving as she had left, to seek better times.

If she had a lot of money, she could buy a fine house, one of the grand old places she had admired since she was a child. She could open a business.

But what good would it do?

She knew enough about business to know that success breeds success and that failure, alas, breeds failure. Bringing even a million dollars to her hometown would do nothing to restore the valley to the way it was when she was younger. Perhaps the bloom she remembered was itself the illusion of youth thinking that it was being nurtured in a perfect place.

If there was a great amount of money coming to her from the sale of the Rose, she would be foolish to invest here. She could invest it where her fingers and toes didn't ache in the cold, where she did not see her breath in the air.

No, she'd go back to Florida, if for no other reason than to return to the print shop and earn a living. Maybe she had learned something from all this.

Cort called her every other night or so, talking briefly of what he was doing and how much he missed her.

Jean found no graceful way of asking him the questions that nagged her more each time she hung up the phone. Perhaps if she held her tongue, she would have some advantage to work with later.

The hurt would not go away.

Chapter Eleven

Cort craned his neck to catch a glimpse of Jean as the passengers deplaned. Just as he began to fear she hadn't caught this flight for some reason, there she was.

She looked surprised to see him, as though she hadn't expected anyone she knew to be in the waiting area. With her duffel bag in her hand, Kiki's leather coat draped over her arm, and her eyes heavy, she looked travel-weary.

Any words he could have said stuck in Cort's throat, and Jean did not seem to have anything to say, either. He reached for the handle of her bag, then embraced her.

Jean raised her head to speak, but he covered her mouth with his. He kissed her with the ardor their days apart had built into a mountain of dried kindling, waiting for the torch of their meeting.

Cort didn't want the kiss to end. He didn't want to hear what she had learned, that the passion growing in him was hopeless and forbidden.

Jean pulled back from him, gasping for breath. He realized where he was. This was a public place, and he was acting in a manner that might cause both of them embarrassment. Yet his hand clung to the pink knit fabric of her T-shirt as though he would never let go.

"I almost didn't recognize you without the black eye," Jean said, breathless.

Cort laughed and tilted his head. "Your suntan is fading."

"I . . . I expected . . . maybe Denise."

"She had to work until five," Cort told her, moving slightly to allow someone to pass them. "I'll take you to your apartment. You can collect everything there and come stay with me at the mansion."

Jean tilted her head, and he knew she objected to the suggestion. She looked around them and began to walk with the flow of people.

"There are a lot of things we have to talk about."

"Yes," he agreed. "Do you have more bags?"

"No." Jean shook her head, which made her long blond hair dance across her shoulders. "Please, I want to go straight to my place. I've been up since I don't know when. The weather's been awful, the flight was bumpy, and I just want to collapse."

"But you will have dinner with me tonight," Cort urged.

Jean sighed.

He had a feeling she was about to argue. "You do have to eat," he pointed out.

Jean chuckled. "My stepmother had the same line, Cort. I haven't been starving."

"Humor me," he pleaded. "Mrs. Ghent and I have been planning this all day."

"When did you get in?" Jean asked.

"Yesterday morning. I am all rested from my trip, and have my jet lag all in hand."

"I wish I could claim jet lag," Jean said, shaking her head.

José was waiting for them in front of the terminal, calmly conversing with another chauffeur as he stood at the rear door of the car.

Jean smiled at him and watched as he opened the door for her. Cort sensed that Jean was becoming more accustomed to letting other people do things for her. It was all to the good. If she accepted his proposal, she was going to find many things being done for her.

Jean settled into the back seat of the car and ran her hand over her face in a tired gesture. He wanted to take her into his arms and erase her fatigue with his kisses, but he restrained himself. There would be time later.

On the way to her apartment he asked her unimportant questions about her trip home and the flight. He asked about everything except what he wanted to know, what he was afraid to hear. She seemed no more willing to tell him specific bits in answer to his inane questions than he was to express what was uppermost in his mind.

It must be the worst, he told himself. *That must be why she's stalling.*

Telling José to wait at the curb in front of the deli, Cort carried Jean's bag up to the apartment for her.

"José will be back for you at seven," Cort told her. "That should give you enough time to pack everything to bring to Pieter's."

"What?" Jean demanded.

"I have only a few days," he explained. "I want you to stay with me."

"Oh, Cort," Jean sighed, dropping her purse on the table and looking at a note from Denise. "I don't know who you are anymore. I thought I did, but a friend tried to check on your credentials and . . . Are you sure you exist? That you're not a figment of my imagination?"

"I have no idea what you're talking about," Cort exploded. This was a problem he had not foreseen.

"It's always been at the back of my mind that you could be a very clever, resourceful schemer, just like the man you captured. My friend—he was actually an old boyfriend—tried to check you out through Interpol. He got a very discouraging response."

244

"I can't believe it!" Cort exclaimed.

The apartment door opened, and Denise breezed in, already talking. He stood staring at Jean and Denise as they hugged and exchanged greetings that were nonsense to him.

Running his hand through his hair, he tried to think how her friend had gotten such a response from the agency. Of course she would be upset if she thought he was a fraud. But how had it happened?

"Jean!" he interrupted. "Will you have enough time to get ready for dinner by seven?"

"What?" Jean asked, her attention divided between Denise's rapid-fire chatter and searching for something on the cluttered table.

"Seven will be fine," Denise assured him, stopping midsentence. "I'll see that she's ready."

"But—" Jean protested. "Cort, we have to talk."

"At dinner," he promised, touching her shoulder briefly and leaving.

Cort walked slowly down the steps from the apartment and returned to his car. Just when he thought he had everything under control, there was one more obstacle to overcome—at least.

"What is this all about?" Jean demanded of Denise when the door had barely closed behind Cort.

"Cort came over last night and told me that

he wanted to plan a dinner for you for tonight," Denise said, taking a can of soda from the refrigerator. "Formal."

"What! Denise!"

"Will you please calm down?" Denise demanded, opening the can and taking a long swallow. "All right. I took the black dress and the blue dress back to the shop where I got them and got you the most beautiful gown they had. Wait until you see it!"

"Great," Jean growled, picking up her duffel to carry it into her room. "Just great. I'm tired and I'm trying to kick this sore throat I caught up home. Now you and whoever Cort is are trying to engineer a social occasion."

"It's just the two of you," Denise told her, following Jean into the bedroom. "Look at this."

Jean was looking. A pale-pink chiffon gown hung from the closet door. Its silver and iridescent beads reflected every nuance of the late-afternoon sun streaming through the window. She took a deep breath and turned the hanger so she could see the back.

"Whew!" she breathed.

"All it takes is confidence," Denise assured her.

"Ha!" Jean laughed. "Denise, you know that I have my doubts about Cort. I'm not about to—"

"Be reasonable! He came back, didn't he?"

246

"Yes . . ."

"Go shower and do your hair. I'll unpack for you." Denise unzipped Jean's duffel bag and began to remove the pouch in which Jean carried her makeup.

"There's a file folder in there that I need to take with me," Jean informed her. "It's private stuff. I'd prefer you not read it."

"You would say that!" Denise teased. "Now it will bother me for the rest of my life."

"Promise you won't read it," Jean pleaded as she opened her lingerie drawer.

She was surprised when Denise capitulated without another word on the subject.

"I'll be too busy helping you get ready," Denise said with a laugh.

José knocked at the door at exactly seven o'clock. Jean took a deep breath and adjusted a bobby pin holding the ambitious arrangement of her hair on the top of her head. Denise had spent fifteen minutes working at it and had pronounced the effect of coiffure and gown perfect.

Now a vague hint of a smile in José's eyes confirmed it. Of course, his was not the opinion that mattered.

Jean dropped Kiki's leather coat over her arm and picked up the file folder and her sequined purse. It was the moment to do or die.

"You won't need a coat, ma'am," José said

respectfully. "It's going to be quite warm this evening."

"But I'm returning it," Jean explained.

"Oh," José said, reaching to take it from her.

Jean followed him, remembering that José's duty was to take care of things, and she had seen plenty of evidence of his proficiency.

The car rolled through the darkened, palm-lined avenues toward the mansion. Jean took great care in holding her hands still in her lap so that she would not bite her thumbnails. She'd spent twenty precious minutes on her nails; she wasn't going to destroy them because of a few frayed nerves.

José drove through the open gates of the mansion far enough to clear them, then got out to close them. When he returned to the car, he took a moment to look back at Jean.

"Ma'am, dinner is being served in the garden room tonight," he told her. "Would you prefer to go in that way or through the front door?"

Jean considered his face for a moment, and realized he was showing her a lot of sympathy. He knew the double front door and the fancy foyer intimidated her. She chose to spend her free moments in the house staring out the garden room windows at the ocean.

"I would rather go in through the garden room, yes," she told him, grateful for his suggestion.

He pulled the car around to the apron of the

garage and walked silently ahead of her, carrying Kiki's coat and the file folder. She had not been quick enough to wrest the folder from his grasp when he slipped it from her hand.

Through the long windows of the garden room, Jean could see Cort lighting the two candles on the small round table. He was wearing his tuxedo, and the collar and cuffs of his white shirt almost gleamed in the soft candlelight. He was an extremely handsome man, she realized again with the same impact of her first glimpse of him.

José stood with his hand on the doorknob, waiting for her to come closer so the sudden breeze of opening the door would not blow out the candles.

Jean straightened her shoulders, raised her chin, and smiled. Whatever happened tonight would be right, she told herself. If she left Cort here, never to see him again, it would be her decision. If she promised him forever, that would be her choice, too.

Distracted by a sound beyond the wall of windows, Cort glanced away from the candles he was lighting. He almost forgot to wave the flame of the match out before it singed his fingers.

"Incredible," he breathed as Jean entered the room. He had never seen her look so elegant, even the night they had met.

She smiled a bit uncertainly, then turned to José, who had entered the room behind her and quickly closed the door.

"I, uh, brought Kiki's coat with me," she stammered. "I should mail it back to her, but she didn't give me her address."

"I'll take care of that," Cort assured her. "Later."

José left the file folder on one of the extra chairs beside the serving credenza and left the room.

Cort and Jean were alone. Finally. But what should have been the rapturous feeling of being reunited was marred by a slight immobility in Jean's expression. It was as though she had lost the trust she'd had in him.

He wondered if she sensed his apprehension at what she had found during her search for the truth about her great-grandmother and how she had acquired the Rose.

Cort shook himself from the inertia of difficult thoughts and moved to the credenza, where a bottle of champagne was chilling in a silver urn.

"We have something to celebrate," he announced, lifting the bottle from the bed of ice and securing a heavy white napkin around it. The cork popped sharply between his thumbs. He tipped the bottle toward the waiting tulip-shaped glasses before any liquid had frothed and spilled onto the silver tray. He returned the bottle to the ice before handing a glass to Jean. "Something to drink to," he told her, taking the other glass.

"Oh?" she asked.

"To the successful sale of the Champagne Rose," he toasted, touching the rim of his glass to hers with a discreet ringing sound.

"Ah!" she exclaimed, then took a sip. "Do you know who bought it?"

Cort took a healthy swallow of the champagne and squared his shoulders. "There was a very famous actress at the auction who wanted it desperately. But after spirited bidding, the son of one of the royal princesses of the Netherlands was successful."

"A prince?" Jean asked, breathless.

"No, a duke. But he doesn't use his title. He works for his living. You may be surprised to know that Dutch royalty are largely sensible that way, possibly because of their experiences in the first half of the century. But the duke is a connoisseur of such things as art and gems," he explained.

"I'm impressed," Jean told him, smiling with her eyes.

Cort reached into an inner pocket of his jacket, bypassed the cloth pouch there, and took out a small envelope. "This may impress you even more," he said, handing it to her.

Jean put her glass down on the table and

took the envelope from him. She ripped it open with eager fingers and extracted a small book.

"That's a numbered account in a Swiss bank in Geneva," he said. "Do you want me to translate the francs to dollars for you?"

"Maybe you'd better."

"It's roughly one million, seven hundred thousand dollars," he reckoned.

Wide-eyed, she whistled softly.

"I chose a Swiss account so that you'll be free to make decisions about your future without worrying about any unusual national banking laws," he explained.

Jean closed the book and shoved it back into its envelope. "I suppose I could do anything I wanted to do now, and no one would question my motives."

"Within reason," Cort cautioned.

"Don't spoil my moment!" she exclaimed, then laughed.

"We Dutch have a way of doing that, too," Cort said apologetically.

Jean dropped the envelope to the table and picked up her glass again, raising it in his direction. "I must say you have eased some of my doubts. Now, are you an Interpol agent or not?"

"Technically I am," Cort said, after another swallow of champagne. "Then again, I'm not. That technicality is probably why your friend didn't get the response you'd hoped for when he made his inquiry. I'm no longer a field agent, but I'm still working with the agency. I'll be assigned a desk and a classroom. That will be much safer."

"Is that what you want?"

"I want to live a long life. I've discovered a reason for living."

He pulled a chair away from the table and motioned for Jean to sit down. "We ought to start on our dinner or Mrs. Ghent will complain that her baked chicken with apricot dressing will be cold and her endive salad will wilt."

Throughout dinner Jean seemed intent on extracting every detail of his work from him. She quizzed him on what he knew of Stefano DePesca's and Simon's fates, and what his new duties would entail. But Cort wanted to know what she had learned at home.

"Was your father well?" he finally asked, crossing his knife and fork on his empty dinner plate and motioning for José to remove it.

"Yes, very," Jean replied. "I was surprised at how well he and Shirley have adjusted to each other. I came to terms with their relationship while I was there. Maybe it was a good thing that I had to stay longer than I'd planned. My father wouldn't let me leave while my cold was so bad. It gave us plenty of time to talk."

"Did you find out about your great-grandmother?" Cort asked, trying to say the words as though the course of his entire life did not depend on her answer. "José, would you ask Mrs.

Ghent to bring the coffee with our dessert?"

Yes, he knew he was stalling, but the order removed José from the room. If he was going to react badly, at least he would not do so in front of his man.

Jean got up from the table, and he started to stand, also, but Jean waved her hand at him to remain seated.

"I swear, you're too much a gentleman, Cort," she said chuckling. "I just want to get this folder so I can prove to you . . ." She opened the folder and glanced down at the contents, tracing what she read with her finger. "Yes, here it is." She sat down across from him once more and looked up at him with pride in her green eyes.

Before she began to read again, José came back from the kitchen and placed a slice of fresh strawberry pie in front of her. Jean held the folder to her chest and smiled. "That's lovely. Thank you."

Cort fidgeted and watched as José served him.

"Anyway, Delia and Tom Finney were married in June 1925, and they didn't have a child until September of '26," Jean said. She handed the document she had been reading across the table to Cort. "Now, the young woman Delia Baker was supposed to be—I don't know how you say this—the woman she was employed to be maid for was Helene McClellan."

"Land sakes!" Mrs. Ghent's voice boomed from the kitchen doorway. "Delia Baker and Helene McClellan! I hadn't thought of them in years." She brought the coffeepot into the room and placed it on the credenza.

Cort and Jean turned surprised faces toward the cook.

"What do you know about them?" Cort asked, pushing his chair back slightly.

"The McClellans rented the house next door every season for years," Mrs. Ghent said, pouring coffee while José hovered. "Back then there were three major reasons to come to Palm Beach. Aside from escaping the cold northern winters, they liked to marry off their children and gossip. I was a little thing of seven or eight when Delia came with them. My father and sister were working here then, and Mama was about to have Jacob, so I remember it all very well. My sister and I thought Delia was wonderful, and lucky to be serving a young woman. Mr. Pieter's grandfather Per and Mr. Cort's grandpa Jan-Wilhelm were very self-sufficient. As I recall, it was Per who was out on the seawall one late afternoon with Miss Helene. She was supposed to be getting ready to go to dinner with—Oh, what was his name . . . Randolph something. Her mama was bound that she was going to marry him."

"Thomas Randolph!" Jean crowed. "Yes!

They were married at the end of the summer in Newport."

"Well, you see." Mrs. Ghent had satisfied herself with her recollection. She seemed ready to return to the kitchen, then remembered that she was telling a story. "Oh, well, Mr. Randolph was driving up in his automobile—oh, it was sporty. Delia saw him and went running out to the seawall to get Miss Helene. At about the same time the Billings yacht was passing just out there. With Rosalie on board!"

"Pieter's grandmother," Cort explained for Jean's benefit.

"Well, to avoid two horrendous scandals," Mrs. Ghent continued, "when the smoke had cleared, Delia swore to all the offended mamas and daddies that she had been on the seawall kissing Mr. Jan-Wilhelm. Old Mr. McClellan threatened to send her home to Pennsylvania on the train. Mrs. van Roy took Delia to her dressing room and offered her something as a reward for being so brave. My sister stood right outside the door and watched through the crack. Delia asked for the silver rose pin that Mrs. van Roy was wearing, but Madam didn't think it was good enough. So Madam picked up the first thing her hand came to—that big diamond pin—and handed it to Delia. Delia told my sister that she didn't really like it as much as she liked the silver rose. But she took it and thanked Madam for it because you daren't cross someone of Madam's position. Mr. McClellan didn't send Delia home just then, though. She stayed the rest of the season. We've often wondered what became of her in the years since."

"She was my great-grandmother," Jean stated simply.

"Well, don't that beat all?" Mrs. Ghent marveled, already on her way back to the kitchen.

Jean settled into her chair and picked up her fork, a devilish smile playing on her lips.

"All right," Cort capitulated. "What are you going to say?"

"I feel that the aspersions you cast on my great-grandmother's character has been vindicated," Jean proclaimed.

"If I had kept up on my English as I should have, I might know whether to agree with you or not."

"Agree with me," Jean advised. She leveled her gaze at him.

"All right, I agree with you." Cort laughed.

Their eyes met. The candles flickered, burnt down to half the length they had when he had lit them.

Neither he nor Jean could address the strawberry pie with much enthusiasm.

"I have something for you," Cort said, reaching into his jacket pocket.

Jean eyed the piece of jewelry he offered her suspiciously as she turned it over in her hand.

257

"This isn't the real Rose," she appraised with relief.

"Right. It's just a pretty piece of glass, prepared by one of the best paste artists in the world. Look on the back."

"An infinity sign with a C and a J," Jean read. "How sweet. I . . . I wish I had a gift for you."

"It doesn't matter," Cort said, leaning across the table to kiss her.

Jean was stunned by the speed with which everything had happened. "I . . . I need to . . . catch my breath," she said.

"I think we both do." Cort stood and held her chair while she got to her feet.

Somewhere the telephone rang twice. José came to the door and motioned for Cort to follow him.

"It's Mr. Pieter," José whispered.

Jean let out her breath as she watched after Cort. His abruptness was something she would definitely have to adjust to, but somehow it was such a part of him that she did not mind.

She sat down at the table once more and took a few small bites of her pie. But then she let the fork slip to the edge of the fine china plate and pushed her dessert away.

Slowly she picked up the fake Rose from where it lay on the tablecloth and got to her feet once more. Thoughtfully she traced the lines of the jewelry with her fingertips, then pinned it to the front of her gown.

After looking at her image in the window, Jean stood staring out at the ocean for a long while.

She saw Cort's reflection before she heard his footsteps behind her.

Gently he placed his hands on her shoulders and drew her to him. His lips touched her neck.

Cort's hands slid down her arms, and he surrounded her with his strength. "I was talking to Pieter," he told her. "They're flying down early tomorrow to spend the weekend."

Jean turned within his embrace so that she could see his face. "Why are they doing that?"

Cort shrugged. "To meet with a real estate agent and decide which personal things should be shipped to their home up north."

"Oh? They can just drop everything and jet down here in their private plane. It must be nice."

"Very nice. I want you to stay here tonight," Cort told her firmly.

Jean was sorely tempted. Yet she shook her head slowly but decisively.

Cort tried to persuade her with a kiss, and with another . . . and another.

"No, Cort. I'm very tired and very confused. I didn't expect you to be here when I came back. And the money! I can't even comprehend what it's going to mean to me. And to us." She placed her hands on the pleated front of his shirt and looked squarely into his eyes. "Is there an us?"

"Yes, my darling. You know that. From the moment I met you, I've known our lives are forever intertwined, both in the past and in the future."

"The future," she mused. "Yes. I love you, Cort."

"I don't know how I could have imagined I loved anyone before. You're all I think about," he assured her.

"But this is not the frame of mind I want to be in the first time we—"

He touched a finger to her lips. "We don't have to . . ."

"If I stayed the night, we would. It wouldn't be right. I'm not ready yet," Jean said, tapping a finger against her forehead.

"All right, then." Cort groaned, letting her go. "After we've had another cup of coffee, I'll take you back to your apartment."

Chapter Twelve

Denise succumbed to anxiety, worried about Jean's dinner date with Cort. She had been speechless the night before when Cort had appeared in the hallway. He'd come back!

She'd wanted to call Jean in Pennsylvania and warn her, but Cort had sworn her to secrecy before outlining his plans for this evening. The guy was a born romantic, of all things. You could forgive a sensitive man almost anything.

Cort had given her some money to buy Jean a gown. In that moment, Denise gained a respect for Cort.

He'd already decoded Jean's character enough to know there was nothing in her wardrobe for a formal occasion, no matter how private. Nor would Jean spend money on something suitable for herself; her priorities were much too basic. Give Jean two hundred bucks and she chipped in for rent and groceries. If she had any left over, it went into the poor box of the church on the corner.

Denise had taken the cash, knowing what she wanted for Jean, and the two dresses she could trade for it wouldn't be enough. Besides, Jean needed something classy she could keep. She was going to be rich, very rich!

One sure cure for her edgy mood tonight was to spend a little money on herself, Denise reasoned. She stuffed a few dollars into the kangaroo pocket of her brown hooded sweatshirt, then headed for the drugstore down the block. A magazine would help her get through the evening while she waited for Jean to return.

Not bothering to put on lipstick, she pulled her hood over her wiry dark hair. Maybe that was why the old lady in front of Denise at the checkout shied away from her.

Denise grinned to herself. Her punk days were long over, but it did gave her a boost to think she might still look younger than she was.

She paid for the fashion magazine, rolled it, and shoved it into the pocket of the sweatshirt. She liked to have her hands free when she was on the street at night.

The elderly woman was just reaching the exit, carrying grocery bags in both arms. Denise pushed the door open for her and waited for her to hobble out into the night.

"You ought to get a good grip on that purse," Denise advised, since it was dangling from the woman's elbow.

"Not much else to do with it," was the grumbled response.

"How far do you have to walk?" Denise asked, fitting the keys to the apartment and her car between her fingers.

"Just over to the Palm Rest House," she said, naming a retirement hotel a block away.

"I could walk with you," Denise offered, peripherally aware of three teenage boys loping noisily across the street.

The old woman looked at her suspiciously and shook her head. She had taken only a few steps when one of the boys separated from the other two, ran across the street, and made a grab for the purse.

Denise started after him, flailing her key-studded fist toward his face, accompanying her action with words the woman had probably never uttered.

Tires squealed on the pavement, but Denise pursued the kid into the street, his attention no longer on the senior citizen.

God! I'm not a kid any more, Denise thought as her lungs began to ache.

"Freeze right there!" A man's deep voice filled the air. A car door slammed, then another.

Denise tried to kick the kid, but he backed away too quickly, and she fell to the pavement.

"My God! That's Denise!" Jean shouted to

Cort and José, recognizing her roommate's sweatshirt.

The men were already out of the car, going to the aid of the combatant who had fallen backward. The three teens scattered, their feet thudding on the pavement.

Jean hitched up the skirt of her beaded gown a few inches and squirmed across the seat to the door of the car.

"It's Denise!" she yelled when Cort motioned for her to stay put. She broke away from his grasp and hurried to her friend.

An old woman with a bewildered expression was standing over Denise. The manager of the drugstore dashed from the doorway, his unbuttoned blue smock fluttering in the breeze. He crouched to examine Denise's head.

"Did you hit your head?"

Denise blinked her dark eyes.

"Are you all right?" the woman asked.

Denise took a couple breaths. "Yeah! Are you? He didn't get your purse, did he?"

"No, ma'am," the woman proclaimed.

Denise tried to get up and slumped back to the ground before Jean and the manager could steady her.

"You all come inside," he said. "I want to be sure you're all right."

Jean felt something around her shoulders. It was Cort's jacket, still holding his warmth as it shielded her from the night air.

It was Cort who took charge, suggesting that José walk the elderly woman home, then calling the police to report the incident.

A few minutes later Denise sat on a chair in the waiting area of the prescription department. Clutching her roommate's trembling hand, Jean stood by anxiously, watching as the pharmacist shone a light in her eyes.

"I'm guessing you're okay, miss, but you should check in with your doctor as soon as possible. Do you have someone to stay with tonight? Someone who can check on you every hour or so?"

"I can do that," Jean volunteered.

Then she caught a dark look from Cort. He apparently didn't think much of the idea.

Jean picked up the magazine Denise had taken from her pocket and put it on the chair beside her. "Come on, Denise," she urged, "we'll get you home and make you comfortable."

José had returned by then and offered his arm to Denise. Cort followed them to the front door.

"Jean," he said in soft urgency, "you can't stay in this neighborhood another night."

"I can't leave Denise!"

"Bring her with you," he suggested as they went out into the darkness of the street.

Jean clutched Cort's jacket to her body. "You wouldn't mind?"

"Yes, I'd mind," he muttered. "But I can't

leave you here tonight, either. God! I hate the thought of you living in this neighborhood!"

Jean stopped walking abruptly and laid her hand on his arm. "Cort, your obsession with security is understandable."

"I've seen some terrible things," he assured her.

"I know and I love you for your concern. But I'm a reasonable person, darling. I don't want to take risks any more than you want me to, not this kind."

Jean raised her chin and hurried toward the apartment over the deli, her hand clasped in his. "I don't have to live here anymore, do I? I can live almost anywhere now."

She had to lift the hem of her dress so that she could maneuver the steps up to the apartment. While they waited for Denise to unlock the door in the dimly-lit hallway, Jean handed Cort's jacket back to him.

"Come on, Denise," she ordered. "Throw a few things in a bag and we'll stay over at the van Roys' tonight."

"Don't be silly," Denise admonished, but a tremor in her voice belied her bravado. "I'll be fine."

"We have plenty of room," Cort told her.

Jean smiled back at him, knowing that his enthusiasm was less than complete. She paused to kiss his cheek, and he wrapped his arm around her to hold her close for just a moment.

"I'll have to take my own car," Denise grumbled, "because I have to go to work tomorrow."

"No," José said. "I'll drive your car. Mr. van Roy can drive the other."

Cort's scowl lifted perceptibly.

They sat at the table in the kitchen, everyone less formal now in jeans and sweaters, enjoying slices of Mrs. Ghent's strawberry pie. Neither Cort nor Denise had seemed to object when Jean asked José to join them for the late-night snack.

When the table was cleared, Denise joked that they should play some poker. She produced a deck of cards from a drawer, and soon they were all engrossed in the game. They used toothpicks instead of cash and Jean observed that a bump on the head didn't dull Denise's skill.

"I guess you're going to be all right, eh?" Jean said, placing her hand on her friend's shoulder.

"Right as rain," Denise agreed, pushing the toothpicks away from her place and getting to her feet. "If you don't mind, I'm going up to our room and take a hot bath."

"I'll be along shortly," Jean told her.

When Jean turned back, she found she and Cort were alone; José had discreetly disappeared.

They walked slowly through the mansion, turning off the lights and making certain that the doors were locked.

"Pieter and Kiki offered me first refusal on this house," Cort told her when they paused in the foyer. "I told them I couldn't afford it right now."

Jean shrugged.

"I find I'm making plans, and I haven't even asked you to marry me."

She chuckled. "I know I love you.

"But you're still not sure that I am who I say I am?"

Jean nodded.

"I'll call the office tomorrow and find out why they didn't tell your friend who I am."

She was going to tell him it didn't matter, but it did.

Before they parted for the night, Cort took both her hands in his. "I understand your need for a little time to think about me and your money and how you must come to terms with everything. I won't pressure you. Tomorrow evening, we'll talk."

"Yes," Jean agreed, relieved.

But there were other problems, she realized, when she and Denise lay in twin beds in the darkness in an upstairs guest room.

"Is the money going to come between us?"

Denise asked bluntly after Jean divulged the approximate sum in her Swiss account.

"Why should it?"

"I've seen how things have already changed," she said. "You aren't as timid about speaking up and doing things your way."

"About tonight? I did what had to be done, Denise. It doesn't mean I want to boss you around."

"Are you sure?"

"Yes, and I want you to share in my good fortune," Jean said. "You've had two years of business college and retail experience. Would you like a shop of your own?"

"I'll think about it," Denise promised, then yawned. "I have to go to work in a few hours."

"Get some sleep," Jean told her. Denise was all right. If their relationship had changed, it was for the better.

Cort had not foreseen having a houseful of people this weekend. Mrs. Ghent wasn't available to cook for them, but he'd expected José to pick up the slack. Jean stepped into the void, getting to the kitchen before José appeared.

She had made coffee and toast for breakfast, but Denise and Cort had not seemed to mind the light fare. Cort laughed at Jean's fretting, joking that there would probably be more than enough food around the house later in the day.

Denise reluctantly left for work, promising to tell her boss of the events the night before and take off if her headache returned.

Cort holed up in the library on the telephone until he had to leave to collect Pieter and Kiki from the airport.

Now there were a few minutes of quiet Jean could claim for herself. It was a perfect morning, she decided as she gazed at the sea through a kitchen window. Watching the waves could be wonderfully relaxing. After a while she collected the dishes from the table and washed them. There was so little to do.

As she dried her hands, she wondered what Cort's home was like, if it was an apartment or a house.

But with her money she could buy them a nice place to live in, no matter what. As a child, she had thought people in Europe lived backward lives, based on her study of history. Then she had seen some magazines left in Levi Freeman's deli. In the photos the plumbing was ultramodern, the furniture futuristic. The prospect of seeing Europe intrigued her.

Knowing that it would be needed soon, Jean started another pot of coffee. The beans were of an aromatic blend she adored. Before, Jean could never afford the price, even a tiny packet for a special dinner.

Yes, that was what she would do with some of the money—put it toward small luxuries.

The rest she'd invest. When it grew, she'd go back home. Then she would be able to make a difference in the lives of people in the hills of Pennsylvania.

Hearing a car in the drive, she hurried to meet Kiki and Pieter, and instantly fell in love with another van Roy man, little Willie.

"I brought your coat back," Jean told Kiki when the men had gone off somewhere. "I don't know where José put it, though."

"Don't worry about it," Kiki said casually and reached for the coffeepot. "Did you get your dress cleaned?"

"Uh, no."

"It was ruined, wasn't it? The stains were too big."

Jean nodded. She'd tried several different methods, but she could still see the discoloration.

"How was the trip home?" Kiki asked, filling two cups.

"It was cold and discouraging, but everything turned out all right," Jean told her, picking up her cup and savoring the delicious flavor.

"I liked your father from what I saw of him," Kiki mused. "He was really glad to see you. I can't think my father would ever be that pleased to see me."

"Don't you get along?" Jean asked, afraid she

was once again intruding.

"It isn't that. It's more that he didn't care. He had my brother to spoil and dote on, and my mother had me. He made Tony into a football player, and she made me into a millionaire's wife."

Jean frowned.

Kiki nodded. Her voice had an uncomfortable bitterness about it. "That was the way it was. They made us into what they wanted us to be." She took a swallow of her coffee and then pushed the cup away. "I didn't understand it all until Pieter got shot. That put everything into a different perspective. I kept wondering what I would have done if he had been killed. I wondered if I would have survived. Socially, I wouldn't have, you know. All I am is Pieter van Roy's wife. I'm no one on my own. I decided that I have to change that somehow. I don't know whether it's something inside or outside that has to change. But I think I have the opportunity."

"If . . . if I married Cort, would I be—"

Kiki looked back at her levelly. "You're your own person, Jean. You wouldn't flinch when you face the cats in the ladies' room. I like you, you know. We could be good friends. We will be!"

As though they were sisters, they reached for each other's hands.

"Now," Kiki proposed, getting to her feet,

"let's go shopping."

"Can we go fishing?" Willie begged, gazing up at his father hopefully.

"There's probably nothing to catch," Pieter told him briskly. "Besides, the boat has already been taken to the marina."

"We could go look at the water," Willie suggested.

"We sure could," Cort agreed, suddenly getting to his feet. "We'll get the poles and take them along just in case we see some fish."

He understood Willie's anxiousness to be out in the fresh air. Why should they fly to Florida from Connecticut if they didn't take advantage of a lovely, warm day?

They strolled out to the seawall and down to the dock. Willie scampered ahead, carrying a pole and a bait pail. Pieter sank his hands into the pockets of his windbreaker and lagged behind Cort's long strides.

Soon Cort set Willie to lowering the pail into a tide pool in an attempt to trap some unsuspecting creature to use as bait. Cort thought that Pieter should have been taking the opportunity to work with his son.

Once Willie was occupied, Cort followed Pieter back up to the seawall.

"How is the arm?" Cort asked, thinking perhaps it was pain and stiffness that bothered Pieter.

"Coming along," Pieter answered without expression.

"Then what's wrong?" Cort demanded, switching to Dutch. If Pieter had something to say that he didn't want Willie to hear, the boy wouldn't understand.

"Why? Why Jean?" Pieter asked. "She's not right for you."

"Oh, I think she's very right for me," Cort countered and could not help smiling.

"You're not using your head!"

"Ah, but I am!" Cort argued. "That's what today is about, Pieter. We could have made promises to each other last night, because we know we love each other. But we have backed off a little to think seriously if we can come to an understanding of each other."

"But there is so much at stake, Cort! And she doesn't even have the preparation Kiki had. She'd never be able to cope in our world."

"She did quite well the night you were shot." Cort's anger was rising. "She can learn what fork to use. You cannot teach a person the inner strength, the purity, the awareness Jean has. My mind is made up."

Pieter stared at the ocean for a long time. "I can't dissuade you?"

"No," Cort replied, knowing the smile on his

own face was becoming a permanent fixture.

"I caught something!" Willie called out, hauling up the bait pail. "Come see! Tell me what it is."

Cort loped down to the dock and peered into the bucket. Someday, somewhere, he would be doing this with his own son.

Kiki commandeered the car Cort had rented and drove to a shopping mall. When Jean mentioned that Denise worked at a nearby boutique, Kiki scrapped her plan to visit a chic department store.

"She may as well earn a commission," Kiki declared, making a beeline for the boutique just past the fountain.

Denise turned from straightening garments on a clearance rack when Jean introduced her to Kiki. They sized each other up for a moment. Then Kiki reached for a gold jacket, holding it up to study the detail and the pricc tag.

"Marvelous!" Kiki pronounced. "Would this fit you, Jean?"

She shook her head and picked out a red blazer she'd had her eye on since before Christmas.'

"Uh! The manager is watching," Denise muttered. "Do you want to try that on?"

Completely unfazed, Kiki continued to examine garments for Jean. "And this blouse and those slacks. Do you like them? They're your size, aren't they?"

Jean hesitated when she looked at the tag.

"Come on, you're no fun!" Kiki teased.

"When do you have your lunch break?" Jean asked Denise.

"In about forty-five minutes."

"Meet us somewhere?"

Kiki flicked through the racks. "By the fountain. Oh, this vest is darling."

Denise went back to what she'd been doing with a knowing expression, and Jean obediently followed Kiki to the changing room.

"That makes a great outfit," Kiki appraised a few minutes later. "I hope that makes up for the dress that was ruined."

Jean looked at Kiki in exasperation. "You don't have to do anything for me, certainly not like this. This is too much."

Kiki shook her head. "It gives me a good feeling to buy you something. I've been trying to curb my urge to shop, but this is different. This is something I owe you."

When Kiki took the purchases to Denise to ring up, she reminded her of their lunch date.

Overhearing, the manager nudged Denise away from the register. "Why don't you take your break now," she suggested. "There's a bit of a lull."

The trio strolled to a restaurant Kiki liked where she told the hostess what table they preferred and informed the waitress she wanted everything on one bill.

"Denise, I've been thinking," Jean said, summing up the conversation on the events of the evening before, "that you can't go back to the apartment."

"You won't get any argument from me," Denise agreed, abandoning her long-held defense of the deteriorating area.

"Cort and I discussed that last night," Jean said. "I'm going to look for a nicer place for us. The trouble is that it will be out of the neighborhood. Then I'll need a car. How will I get to work at the print shop?"

Kiki laughed. "You need to change your thinking, Jean. Rent a car until everything is settled between you and Cort. There's no sense in buying one if you're going to be living in Europe soon."

"But that would be so expensive," Jean protested.

"Not really," Kiki observed. "Besides, do you know what the interest on your principle is in a week?"

Jean studied her, wondering how much Kiki knew of her personal finances. "What?"

"Conservatively, the interest on a million dollars is around a thousand dollars a week," Kiki informed her. "You can live on that, can't you?"

Denise's dark eyes widened. "Three families could live on that! You don't have to work,

Jean."

"This is true," Kiki agreed. "But when I married Pieter, I dropped everything I did before. My job, my social life, all my hobbies. I centered my existence around him. I went through a period of total confusion. Keep your job a little longer, phase into your new life in deliberate stages, or you'll forget who you are."

Denise nodded sagely. "That's good advice, and not just for people who are rich."

Jean was surprised that Kiki and Denise were in accord, that they were equally concerned for her future.

"I've made the mistake of living my life with Pieter based on what other people think of me," Kiki revealed. "I need to search out a simpler path to follow, or I'll never find the person I am at heart. You know who you are, and you'd do well to keep the money from obscuring that. You'll need strength to avoid being swept into the current of what other people want from you."

"I want to be very careful with my money," Jean announced. "If Cort and I marry, I want to have a nice home with some of the things he enjoys when he visits you."

Kiki looked at her questioningly. "I don't understand."

"You and Pieter are so generous with him, letting him use your boat and everything."

Kiki pressed her hand to the front of her silk

278

blouse and laughed. "You think he doesn't live like this in Paris? Of course he hasn't told you! Oh, dear, are you in for a shock!"

Late in the afternoon Jean and Kiki made a whirlwind stop at a supermarket. Kiki blithely chose some delicacies Jean had never even considered.

In the rush to take their purchases from the car when they returned to the mansion, Jean could not follow the discussion between Kiki and Pieter. She heard Kiki say, "Denise is getting off work around nine, and we'll discuss it with her then. Now, I'm going to fix a snack for Willie and something to hold us until supper when Denise arrives."

Kiki seemed happy to putter around the kitchen. At one point she turned to Jean and warned, "Don't ever tell Mrs. Ghent that I can cook. It won't make any difference now that we're selling the place, but I've been itching to get my hands on this kitchen. Our housekeeper Hortense went into shock when I invaded her space, but she's adjusted."

They had time to hear Willie play the piano in the magnificent formal living room before he went off to bed. Later, when Denise came, everyone pitched in to lay out a buffet supper in the garden room.

"The girls can't stay there any longer," Kiki

said after a retelling of the events of the night before.

Cort's grim expression reaffirmed a conclusion he had reached long before.

"I think they should stay here, house-sit for us until we sell, or until Jean and Cort resolve their relationship and Denise can find a safer place," Kiki suggested.

Pieter seemed surprised that Kiki had come up with a solution but agreed with her.

"What do you think?" Denise asked Jean.

"If you feel there's enough room for the two of us here," Jean joked. "It's very generous of you both. Yes, we'll do it."

"I'll help you move in tomorrow," Cort offered. "You can get out of your lease, can't you?"

"Levi Freeman will be glad to get rid of us," Denise commented with a covert wink toward Jean. "We're always a week late with the rent!"

After supper Cort took Jean's hand and pulled her along after him out to the patio. A full moon dusted the landscape with silvery light.

"We haven't seen very much of each other today, have we?" he asked, encircling her with his arms and kissing her.

"I think you'll find it was worth the deprivation," Jean said, wrapping her hands behind his neck.

"I've solved the mystery of why the police in your hometown could not get a straight answer to their inquiry about me," he told her. "It was a bureaucratic snarl because my classification had changed so quickly. The clerk in charge tried to get a clearance to tell your friend who I was, but the papers were misfiled."

"I'm sorry you had to go to the trouble," Jean apologized.

Then he groaned and looked up into the sky. "Jean, I've got to stop lying to you."

"What!" she gasped.

"Interpol wouldn't have verified my identity in a hundred requests, for security reasons. My father is the Netherlands' ambassador to France. When I called the bureau this morning, I was told your friend's request was ignored for that reason."

"Is that really the truth?" Jean demanded.

Cort chuckled. "Do you still want to see my passport and my driver's license? My badge again?"

"No, that won't be necessary. I see things much more clearly now."

"Does that mean you've had some time to think?"

"Yes," Jean replied. "I had a chance to think and to listen to Kiki. Tonight my head is telling me that my heart has been right all along."

Cort sat down on the low wall that formed

the boundary between the patio and the lawn and pulled Jean into his lap. "Pieter tried to talk me out of it," he confessed, "but the more he talked, the more I knew we are right for each other."

"Kiki said I'm in for a big shock, and I just can't get that out of my mind. Did she mean about your father?"

"Shock?" Cort asked, acting as though he didn't understand.

"Come on! I've heard you use that word. You know what it means," she scolded. "Don't you ever play dumb with me, because for all your modesty, you know English as well as I do, if not better."

"Oh, I can't think of anything about me that should be a shock to you," Cort said in a playful tone. "What were you talking about at the time?"

"I told her I wanted to provide us with a nice place to live in when we married. She seemed to think that was hilarious."

"That's because I have a very nice apartment, dear. I own the building and use the whole top floor. It has a fantastic view of the Seine."

"So that's all she meant?" Jean asked, touching his cheek.

Suddenly Cort laughed. All the tension she had seen in his face since she had met him evaporated.

He held her more closely. "I have a house in Amsterdam, also, and there's the family home in one of the northern provinces of the Netherlands."

"Does being in Interpol pay that well?"

"I dabble in trading art," Cort told her lightly. "But tonight that's all very far away. You are here, and we should use the time we have together more wisely."

"Yes," Jean agreed. When their lips met, she gave her full attention to sharing his kisses.

After a long moment he broke away slightly. "We must make this official. Will you marry me, and come to Paris to live?"

"Yes!" Jean proclaimed decisively.

"When?"

"Soon!"

Epilogue

"I brought you something," Jean teased when they were finally alone in the study of Cort's Paris apartment.

"In addition to all the people who flew over with you?" he asked, reaching for the drawer of his desk. "What could you possibly have room for?"

Jean giggled.

On the flight from America, in first class, Denise had fretted that all the gowns might end up in Bangkok. She had spent most of her free time in the past few months studying her plans to start an import company to wholesale French accessories to clothing shops in Florida.

Jean's father and his wife, Shirley, had reviewed their plans for a second honeymoon. Pieter and Kiki had made unnecessary apologies for Willie's endless questions. They'd all had a wonderful time.

"I brought you a picture of your grandfather," she announced proudly. "Helene McClellan Randolph's son found it in a photo album."

She took the gift from her purse and handed it to him. "I think you favor him."

"How did you ever come by this?" Cort was stunned as he turned the framed picture to the light.

"Detective work," Jean proclaimed cryptically.

"Well . . ." Cort said, putting the picture aside and pressing a button on his desk. "I was going to wait until the day of our wedding, but I think I should give this to you now to wear on your wedding gown."

He moved the Matisse aside and exposed a wall safe, from which he took a small cloth pouch.

Jean's mouth dropped open when he placed the van Roy Champagne Rose in her hand. The setting had been cleaned and the clasp made more secure. The central stone gleamed in the clear light that spotlighted Cort's art collection.

"Cort," she sighed, almost scolding him. "You said a duke, the son of a royal princess, bought this."

"He did," Cort assured her, a mysterious smile in his gray-gold eyes.

"Did you buy it from him?"

Cort shook his head. "I find my title a burden. I much prefer a life of solving puzzles."

"Are you in line for—"

"Oh, no!" Cort told her. "I'm about sixty-first in line."

"Good! Somehow it makes me feel better that

in marrying a commoner like me, you're not really giving up something you want."

"Even if I were giving up all the world, I would marry you," Cort declared confidently.

"Your mother is a real princess?"

"Well, yes. But my father is a duke in his own right, also. You'll be meeting them tomorrow afternoon."

"Is that the shock Kiki warned me about?"

"Ah, yes, that's probably it. But Mother will love you, as much as I do."

Jean handed the Rose back to him to return to the safe. "Take good care of this," she told him, standing on her tiptoes to kiss him. "Now it means the world to me."

DISCOVER DEANA JAMES!

CAPTIVE ANGEL   (2524, $4.50/$5.50)
Abandoned, penniless, and suddenly responsible for the biggest tobacco plantation in Colleton County, distraught Caroline Gillard had no time to dissolve into tears. By day the willowy red-head labored to exhaustion beside her slaves . . . but each night left her restless with longing for her wayward husband. She'd make the sea captain regret his betrayal until he begged her to take him back!

MASQUE OF SAPPHIRE   (2885, $4.50/$5.50)
Judith Talbot-Harrow left England with a heavy heart. She was going to America to join a father she despised and a sister she distrusted. She was certainly in no mood to put up with the insulting actions of the arrogant Yankee privateer who boarded her ship, ransacked her things, then "apologized" with an indecent, brazen kiss! She vowed that someday he'd pay dearly for the liberties he had taken and the desires he had awakened.

SPEAK ONLY LOVE   (3439, $4.95/$5.95)
Long ago, the shock of her mother's death had robbed Vivian Marleigh of the power of speech. Now she was being forced to marry a bitter man with brandy on his breath. But she could not say what was in her heart. It was up to the viscount to spark the fires that would melt her icy reserve.

WILD TEXAS HEART   (3205, $4.95/$5.95)
Fan Breckenridge was terrified when the stranger found her near-naked and shivering beneath the Texas stars. Unable to remember who she was or what had happened, all she had in the world was the deed to a patch of land that might yield oil . . . and the fierce loving of this wildcatter who called himself Irons.

OFFICIAL ENTRY FORM
Please enter me in the

Lucky in Love

SWEEPSTAKES

Grand Prize choice: _____

Name: _____

Address: _____

City: _____ **State** _____ **Zip** _____

Store name: _____

Address: _____

City: _____ **State** _____ **Zip** _____

MAIL TO: LUCKY IN LOVE
      P.O. Box 1022A
      Grand Rapids, MN 55730-1022A

Sweepstakes ends: 2/26/93

OFFICIAL RULES
"LUCKY IN LOVE" SWEEPSTAKES

1. To enter complete the official entry form. No purchase necessary. You may enter by hand printing on a 3"x5" piece of paper, your name, address and the words "Lucky In Love". Mail to: "Lucky In Love" Sweepstakes, P.O. Box 1022A, Grand Rapids, MN 55730-1022-A.

2. Enter as often as you like, but each entry must be mailed separately. Mechanically reproduced entries not accepted. Entries must be received by February 26, 1993.

3. Winners selected in a random drawing on or about March 12, 1993 from among all eligible entries received by Marden-Kane, Inc. an independent judging organization whose decisions are final and binding. Winner may be required to sign an affidavit of eligibility and release which must be returned within 14 days or alternate winner(s) will be selected. Winners permit the use of their name/photograph for publicity/advertising purposes without further compensation. No transfer of prizes permitted. Taxes are the sole responsibility of the prize winners. Only one prize per family or household.

4. Winners agree that the sponsor, its affiliates and their agencies and employees shall not be liable for injury, loss or damage of any kind resulting from participation in this promotion or from the acceptance or use of the prizes awarded.

5. Sweepstakes open to residents of the U.S., except employees of Zebra Books, their affiliates, advertising and promotion agencies and Marden-Kane, Inc. Void where taxed, prohibited or restricted by law. All Federal, State and Local laws and regulations apply. Odds of winning depend upon the total number of eligible entries received. All prizes will be awarded. Not responsible for lost, misdirected mail or printing errors.

6. For the name of the Grand Prize Winner, send a self-addressed stamped envelope to: "Lucky In Love" Winners, P.O. Box 706-A, Sayreville, NJ 08871.